www.**kidsatrandomhouse**.co.uk

www.lucyandstephenhawking.com

Also available by
Lucy and Professor Stephen Hawking:

GEORGE'S SECRET
KEY TO THE UNIVERSE

*'A dramatic adventure story . . . for
any young cosmologist in the making'*
GUARDIAN

'Miss it at your peril!'
CAROUSEL

GEORGE'S COSMIC TREASURE HUNT

Lucy & Stephen HAWKING

Illustrated by Garry Parsons

DOUBLEDAY

GEORGE'S COSMIC TREASURE HUNT
A DOUBLEDAY BOOK 978 0 385 61190 9
TRADE PAPERBACK 978 0 385 61382 8

Published in Great Britain by Doubleday,
an imprint of Random House Children's Books
A Random House Group Company

This edition published 2009

1 3 5 7 9 10 8 6 4 2

The Random House Group Limited supports the Forest Stewardship Council (FSC),
the leading international forest certification organization. All our titles that are
printed on Greenpeace-approved FSC-certified paper carry the FSC logo.
Our paper procurement policy can be found at www.rbooks.co.uk/environment.

Mixed Sources
Product group from well-managed
forests and other controlled sources
www.fsc.org Cert no. TT-COC-2139
© 1996 Forest Stewardship Council
FSC

Set in 13.5pt Stempel Garamond

RANDOM HOUSE CHILDREN'S BOOKS
61–63 Uxbridge Road, London W5 5SA

www. lucyandstephenhawking.com
www.**rbooks**.co.uk

Addresses for companies within The Random House Group Limited can be found at:
www.randomhouse.co.uk/offices.htm

THE RANDOM HOUSE GROUP Limited Reg. No. 954009

A CIP catalogue record for this book is available from the British Library.

Printed and bound in Great Britain by Clays Ltd, St Ives plc

For Rose

GEORGE'S
COSMIC TREASURE
HUNT

THE LATEST SCIENTIFIC THEORIES!

There are a number of fabulous science essays that appear within the story to give readers a fascinating real insight into some of the latest theories. These have been written by the following eminent scientists:

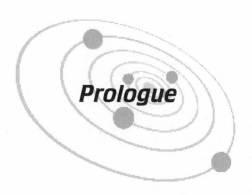

Prologue

'*T minus seven minutes and thirty seconds,*' said a robotic voice. '*Orbiter access arm retracted.*'

George gulped and shifted his bottom in the Commander's seat on the space shuttle. This, finally, was it. There was no getting off the spaceship now. In just a few short minutes – minutes that were ticking by far faster than the endless ones of the last class at school – he'd be leaving planet Earth behind and flying into the cosmos.

Now that the Orbiter access arm, which formed the bridge between his spacecraft and the outside world, had been taken away, George knew he'd missed his final chance to leave. This was one of the last stages before lift-off. It meant the connecting hatches were closing. And they weren't just closing – they were being *sealed*. Now, even if he hammered on the hatches and begged to be let out, there would be no one on the other side to hear him. The astronauts were alone with their mighty spacecraft, with just minutes to go before take-off. There was nothing to do now but wait for the countdown to reach zero.

'*T minus six minutes and fifteen seconds. Perform APU pre-start.*' The APUs – the Auxiliary Power Units – helped to steer the shuttle during launch and landing. They were powered by three fuel cells, which had been running for hours already. But this command made the shuttle hum with life, as though the spaceship knew its moment of glory was not far off now.

'*T minus five minutes,*' said the voice. '*Go for APU start.*'

George's stomach quivered with butterflies. Above all things in the Universe, he wanted to fly through space once more. And now here he was, on board a real spaceship with astronauts inside it, waiting on a launch pad for lift-off. It was exciting but scary at the same time. What if he got something wrong? He was in the Commander's seat, which meant he was in charge of operating the shuttle. Next to him sat his pilot, who was there as the Commander's back-up. 'So, you're all astronauts on some kind of star trek?' he muttered to himself in a silly voice.

'What was that, Commander?' came a voice over George's headset.

'Oh, er, um . . .' said George, who'd forgotten that launch control could hear every word he said. 'Just wondering what aliens might say to us, if we run into any.'

Launch control laughed. 'You be sure to tell them we all said hi.'

'*T minus three minutes and three seconds. Engines to start position.*'

Vroom vroom, thought George to himself. The three engines and the two solid rocket boosters would provide the speed during the first few seconds of lift-off, when the shuttle would be moving at 100 miles per hour before it even cleared the launch tower. It would only take eight and a half minutes to reach a speed of 17,500 miles an hour!

'*T minus two minutes. Close visors.*' George's fingers itched to flip a couple of the thousands of switches in front of him, just to see what would happen, but he didn't dare. In front of him was the joystick that he, the Commander, would use to steer the shuttle once they got into space, and then to dock with the International

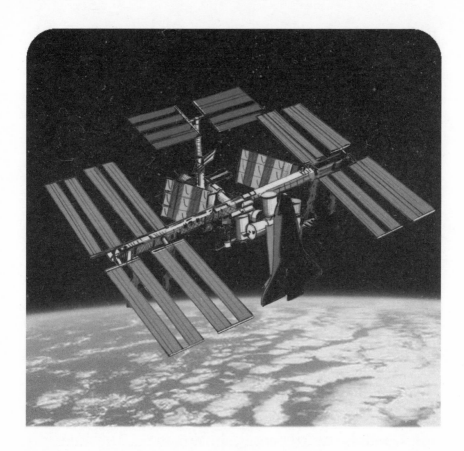

Space Station. It was like being in charge of the steering wheel of a car, except that the joystick moved in all sorts of directions rather than just left and right. It could go backwards and forwards as well. He put one finger on the top of the joystick, just to see what that felt like. One of the electronic graphs in front of him shivered very slightly as he did so. He snatched his hand back and pretended he hadn't touched anything.

'*T minus fifty-five seconds. Perform solid rocket*

booster lock out.' The two solid rocket boosters would blast the space shuttle off the pad and up to around 230 miles above the Earth. They didn't have an 'off' switch. Once they were ignited, the space shuttle was going up.

Goodbye, Earth, thought George. *I'll be back soon.* He felt a twinge of sadness at leaving his beautiful planet, his friends and his family behind. In just a short time he would be orbiting over their heads when the shuttle docked with the International Space Station. He would be able to look down and see the Earth as the ISS whizzed overhead, completing a full orbit once every ninety minutes. From space, he would be able to see the outlines of continents, oceans, deserts, forests and lakes, and the lights of big cities at night. Looking up from Earth, his mum and dad and his friends, Eric, Annie and Susan, would only see him as a tiny bright dot moving fast across the sky on a clear night.

'T minus thirty-one seconds. Ground launcher sequencer go for auto sequence.'

The astronauts wriggled slightly in their seats, wanting to get comfortable before their long journey. Inside the cockpit, it felt surprisingly small and cramped. Just getting into position for take-off had been a squeeze and George had needed the help of a space engineer to clamber into his seat. The space shuttle stood upright for lift-off, so everything in the cockpit seemed as though it had been turned on its bottom. The seat was

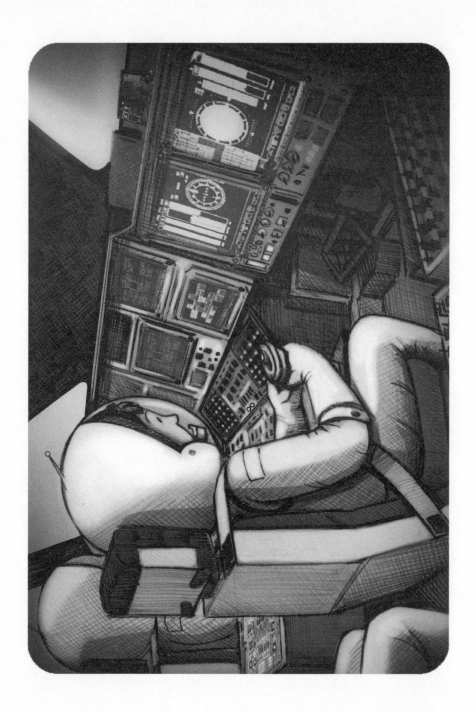

tilted right back so that George's feet were pointing up towards the nose of the shuttle and his spine was in line with the ground underneath.

The shuttle was in rocket mode, waiting to go vertically through the sky, clouds and atmosphere, way up into the cosmos itself.

'*T minus sixteen seconds*,' the robotic voice said very calmly. '*Activate sound suppression water. T minus fifteen seconds.*'

'Take-off minus fifteen seconds, Commander George,' said the pilot in the seat next to George's. 'The space shuttle launches in fifteen seconds and counting.'

'Woo-hoo!' cheered George. *Yikes!* he thought.

'Woo-hoo to you too, Commander,' replied launch control. 'Have a good flight.'

George shivered with excitement. Every breath he took counted down towards the great launch itself.

'*T minus ten seconds. Free hydrogen burn-off system ignition. Ground launcher sequencer go for main engine start.*'

This was it! It was really happening!

Looking out of the window, George could see a strip of green grass and, above it, the blue sky where birds wheeled about. Lying on his back in his astronaut's seat, he tried to feel calm and in control.

'*T minus six seconds*,' said the announcer. '*Main engine start.*' George felt an incredible shaking as the three main engines started, even though the shuttle wasn't yet moving. Through his headset, he heard launch control again.

'*We are go for launch at T minus five seconds and counting. Five, four, three, two, one. You are go for launch.*'

'Yes,' said George very calmly, although inside he was screaming. 'We are go for launch.'

'*T minus zero. Solid rocket booster ignition.*'

The shaking increased. Underneath George and the other astronauts, the two rocket boosters ignited. It was like being kicked sharply in the backside. With a huge roar, the rockets broke through the silence, propelling the space shuttle off the launch pad and up into the skies. George felt as though he had blasted off from Earth while strapped to an enormous firework. Anything could happen now – it could explode; it could veer off course and crash back to Earth or head up into the skies and spin out of control. And there would be nothing George could do about it.

Through the window, he saw the blue of the Earth's atmosphere all around the spaceship, but he could no longer see the Earth itself – he was leaving his own planet! A few seconds after launch and the shuttle performed a roll so that the astronauts were upside down, under the big orange fuel tank!

'Arrrgggghhh!'
yelled George. 'We're
upside down! We're
flying into space the wrong
way up! Help! Help!'
'It's OK, Commander!'
said the pilot. 'We always do
it this way.'

Two minutes after launch George
felt a huge jolt which rocked the whole
spacecraft.

'What was that?' he cried.

Out of the window, he saw first one and then the
second rocket booster detach and fly away from the
shuttle in a great big arc.

It was suddenly quiet now that the rocket boosters
had gone; so quiet it was nearly silent inside the Orbiter.
He looked through the window and wanted to fill the
silence with cheering. The shuttle rolled around again
so that the Orbiter was once more on top of the big
orange fuel tank rather than underneath it.

After eight minutes and thirty seconds in the air
– George felt like entire centuries could have passed by
and he wouldn't have noticed – the three main engines
shut down and the external fuel tank detached.

'There she goes!' whistled his pilot, and through
the window George saw the huge orange fuel tank
disappear from view to burn up in the atmosphere.

Outside, they passed the boundary line where the blue of the Earthly sky turns into the black of outer space. Around them, distant stars shone. They were still climbing higher but they didn't have much further to go before they reached their maximum height.

'All systems are good,' said George's pilot, checking all the flashing lights on the panels. 'Heading for orbit. Commander, will you take us into orbit?'

'I will,' said George confidently, now speaking to mission control in Texas. 'Houston' – he said the most famous word in the history of space travel – 'we are go for orbit. Do you read me, Houston? This is *Atlantis*. We are go for orbit.'

In the darkness outside, the stars suddenly looked very bright and very close. One of them seemed to be zooming towards him, shining a bright light directly into his face, so close and so brilliant that—

He woke up with a start and found himself in an unfamiliar bed with someone flashing a torch in his face.

'George!' the figure hissed. 'George! Get up! It's an emergency!'

Chapter 1

It hadn't been easy to decide what to wear. 'Come as your favourite space object,' he'd been told by Eric Bellis, the scientist next door, who had invited George to his fancy-dress party. The problem was, George had so many favourite outer-space objects he hadn't known which one to pick.

Should he dress up as Saturn with its rings?

Perhaps he could go as Pluto, the poor little planet that wasn't a planet any more?

Or could he go as the darkest, most powerful force in the Universe, a black hole? He didn't think too long or hard about that – amazing, huge and fascinating as black holes are, they didn't really count as his favourite space objects. It would be quite hard to get fond of something that was so greedy it swallowed up anything and everything – including light – that came too close.

In the end George had his mind made up for him. He'd been looking at images of the Solar System on the internet with his dad when they came across a

picture sent back from a Mars rover, one of the robots exploring the planet's surface. It showed what looked like a person standing on the red planet. As soon as he saw the photo, George knew he wanted to go to Eric's party as the Man from Mars. Even George's dad, Terence, got excited when he saw it. Of course, they both knew it wasn't really a Martian in the picture – it was just an illusion caused by a trick of the light that made a rocky outcrop look like a person. But it was exciting to imagine that we might not be alone in this vast Universe after all.

'Dad, do you think there *is* anyone out there?' asked George as they gazed at the photo. 'Like Martians or beings in faraway galaxies? And if there are, do you think they might come and visit us?'

'If there are,' said his dad, 'I expect they're looking at

us and wondering what we must be like – to have this beautiful, wonderful planet and make such a mess of it. They must think we're really stupid.' He shook his head sadly.

Both George's parents were eco-warriors, on a mission to save the Earth. As part of their campaign, up until now electrical gadgets like telephones and computers had been banned from the house. But when George had won the first prize in the school science competition – his very own computer – his mum and dad didn't have the heart to say he couldn't keep it.

In fact, since they'd had the computer in the house, George had shown them how to use it and had even helped them put together a very snappy virtual advert featuring a huge photo of Venus. WHO WOULD WANT TO LIVE HERE? it said in big letters. *Clouds of sulphuric acid, temperatures of up to 470 degrees Celsius . . . The seas have dried up and the atmosphere is so thick, sunlight can't break through. This is Venus. But if we're not careful, this could be the Earth. Would you want to live on a planet like this?* George was very proud of the poster, which his parents and their friends had emailed all around the world to promote their cause.

VENUS

Venus is the brightest object in the sky after the Sun and the Moon. Named after the Roman goddess of beauty, Venus has been known since prehistoric times. Ancient Greek astronomers thought it was two stars, one that shone in the morning, Phosphorus, the bringer of light; and one in the evening, Hesperus, until Greek philosopher and mathematician Pythagoras realized they were one and the same object.

Venus is the second planet from the Sun and the sixth largest in the Solar System.

Venus is often called Earth's twin. It is about the same size, mass and composition as the Earth.

But Venus is a very different world from the Earth.

It has a very thick, toxic atmosphere, mostly made of carbon dioxide with clouds of sulphuric acid. These clouds are so dense that they trap heat, making Venus the hottest planet in the Solar System, with surface temperatures of up to 470 degrees Celsius – so hot that lead would melt there. The pressure of the atmosphere is 90 times greater than Earth's. This means that if you stood on the surface of Venus, you would feel the same pressure as you would at the bottom of a very deep ocean on Earth.

The dense spinning clouds of Venus don't just trap the heat. They also reflect the light of the Sun, which is why the planet shines so brightly in the night sky. Venus may have had oceans in the past, but the water was vaporized by the greenhouse effect and escaped from the planet.

Some scientists believe that the runaway 'greenhouse' effect on Venus is similar to conditions that might prevail on Earth if global warming isn't checked.

Venus is thought to be the least likely place in the Solar System for life to exist.

Since Mariner 2 in 1962, Venus has been visited by space probes more than 20 times. The first space probe ever to land on another planet was the Soviet Venera 7 which landed on Venus in 1970; Venera 9 sent back photos of the surface – but it didn't have long to do it: the space probe melted after just 60 minutes on the hostile planet! The US orbiter, Magellan, later used radar to send back images of the details of the surface of Venus, which had previously been hidden by the thick clouds of its atmosphere.

Venus rotates in the opposite direction from the Earth! If you could see the sun through its thick clouds, it would rise in the west and set in the east. This is called *retrograde* motion; the direction in which the Earth turns is called *prograde*.

A year on Venus takes less time than a day there! Because Venus turns so slowly, it revolves all the way around the Sun in a shorter time than it takes to rotate once on its axis.

One day on Venus
= 243 Earth days

One year
on Venus
= 224.7
Earth days

About twice a century Venus passes between the Earth and the Sun. This is called the *transit of Venus*. These transits always happen in pairs eight years apart. Since the telescope was invented, transits have been observed in 1631 and 1639; 1761 and 1769; and 1874 and 1882. On 8 June 2004 astronomers saw the tiny dot of Venus crawl across the Sun; the second in this pair of early 21st-century transits will occur on 6 June 2012.

Venus spins
on its axis once
every 243
Earth days.

Given what he knew about Venus, George felt pretty sure that there wasn't any life to be found on that smelly, hot planet. So he didn't even consider going to Eric's party dressed as a Venusian. Instead, he got his mum, Daisy, to help him with an outfit of dark orange bobbly clothes and a tall pointy hat so he looked just like the photo of the 'Martian' they'd found.

Wearing his costume, George now waved goodbye to his parents – who had a big evening planned, helping

some eco-friends make organic treats for a party of their own – and squeezed through the gap in the fence between his garden and Eric's. The gap had come about when George's pet pig, Freddy (given to him by his gran), had escaped from his pigsty, barged through the fence and broken into Eric's house via the back door. Following the trail of hoof prints that Freddy had left behind him, George had ended up meeting his new neighbours, who had only just moved into the empty house next door. This chance encounter with Eric and his family had changed George's life for ever.

Eric had shown George his amazing computer, Cosmos, who was so clever and so powerful that he could draw doorways through which Eric, his daughter Annie, and George could walk to visit any part of the known Universe.

But space can be very dangerous, as George found out when one of their space adventures ended with Cosmos exploding from the sheer effort of mounting the rescue mission.

Since that day, Cosmos had stopped working so George hadn't had another chance to step through the doorway and travel around the Solar System and beyond. He missed Cosmos, but at least he had Eric and Annie – he could see them any time he wanted, even if he couldn't go on adventures into outer space with them.

George scampered up the garden path to Eric's back door. The house was brightly lit, with chatter and music pouring out. Opening the door, he let himself into the kitchen.

He couldn't see Annie, Eric or Annie's mum, Susan, but there were lots of other people milling about: one grown-up immediately pushed a plate of shiny silver-iced muffins under his nose. 'Have a meteorite!' he said cheerfully. 'Or perhaps I should say – have a meteoroid!'

'Oh . . . um, well, thanks,' said George, a bit startled. 'They look delicious,' he added, helping himself to one.

'If I did this,' continued the man, tipping some of the buns onto the floor, 'then I could say, "Have a meteorite!" because then they would have hit the ground. But when I offered them to you, suspended in the air, they were – technically – still meteoroids.' He beamed at George and then at the buns, which were lying in a pile on the floor at his feet. 'You get the distinction – a meteoroid is a chunk of rock that flies through the air; a meteor*ite* is what you call that piece of rock if it lands on the Earth. So now I've dropped them on the floor, we can call them meteorites.'

With the bun in his hand, George smiled politely, nodded and started backing away slowly.

'Ouch!' He heard a squeak as he trod on someone behind him.

'Oops!' he said, turning round.

'It's OK, it's only me!' It was Annie, dressed all in black. 'You couldn't have seen me anyway cos I'm invisible!' She swiped the bun out of George's hand and stuffed it into her mouth. 'You only know I'm here because of the effect I have on objects around me. What does that makes me?'

'A black hole, of course!' said George. 'You swallow anything that comes near you, you greedy pig.'

'Nope!' said Annie triumphantly. 'I knew you'd say that but that's wrong! I am' – she looked very pleased with herself – 'dark matter.'

'What's that?' asked George.

'No one knows,' said Annie, mysteriously. 'We can't see it but it seems to be absolutely essential to keep galaxies from flying apart. What are you?'

'Um, well,' said George, 'I'm the man from Mars – y'know, from the pictures.'

'Oh yeah!' said Annie. 'You can be my Martian ancestor. That's cool.'

Around them, the party was buzzing. Groups of the most oddly dressed grown-ups stood eating and drinking and talking at the tops of their voices. One man had come dressed as a microwave oven, another as a rocket. There was a lady wearing a badge shaped like an exploding star and a man with a mini satellite dish on his head. One scientist was bouncing around in a bright green suit, ordering people to 'Take me to your leader'; another was blowing up an enormous balloon stamped with the words THE UNIVERSE IS INFLATING. A man dressed all in red kept standing next to people and then stepping away from them, daring them to guess what he was. Next to him was a scientist wearing lots of different-sized hula-hoop rings around his middle, each one with a different-sized ball attached to it. When he walked, his hula hoops all spun around him.

'Annie,' said George urgently, 'I don't understand any of these costumes. What have they come as?'

'Um, well, they've all come as things you find in space, if you know how to look for them,' said Annie.

'Like what?' asked George.

'Well, like the man dressed in red,' explained Annie. 'He keeps stepping away from people, which means he's pretending to be the redshift.'

'The what?'

'If a distant object in the Universe, like a galaxy, is moving away from you, its light will appear more red than otherwise. So he's dressed in red and he is moving *away* from people to show them he's come as the redshift. And the others have come as all sorts of cosmic stuff that you find out there – like microwaves and faraway planets.'

LIGHT AND HOW IT TRAVELS THROUGH SPACE

One of the most important things in the Universe is the *Electromagnetic Field*. It reaches everywhere; not only does it hold atoms together, but it also makes tiny parts of atoms (called electrons) bind different atoms together or create electric currents. Our everyday world is built from very large numbers of atoms stuck together by the electromagnetic field; even living things, like human beings, rely on it to exist and to function.

Jiggling an electron creates waves in the field – this is like jiggling a finger in your bath and making ripples in the water. These waves are called *electromagnetic waves*, and because the field is everywhere, the waves can travel far across the Universe, until stopped by other electrons that can absorb their energy. They come in many different types, but some affect the human eye, and we know these as the various colours of visible light. Other types include radio waves, microwaves, infrared, ultraviolet, X-rays and gamma rays. Electrons are jiggled all the time – by atoms that are constantly jiggling too – so there are always electromagnetic waves being produced by objects. At room temperature they are mainly infrared, but in much hotter objects the jiggling is more violent, and produces visible light.

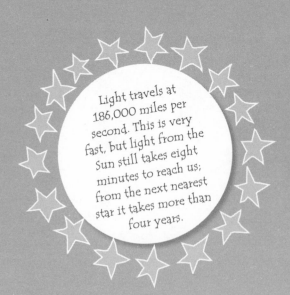

Light travels at 186,000 miles per second. This is very fast, but light from the Sun still takes eight minutes to reach us; from the next nearest star it takes more than four years.

Very hot objects in space, such as stars, produce visible light, which may travel a very long way before hitting something. When you look at a star, the light from it may have been moving serenely through space for hundreds of years. It enters your eye and, by jiggling electrons in your retina, turns into electricity, which is sent along the optic nerve to your brain; and your brain says: 'I can see a star!' If the star is very far away you may need a telescope to collect enough of the light for your eye to detect; or the jiggled electrons could instead create a photograph or send a signal to a computer.

The Universe is constantly expanding, inflating like a balloon. This means that distant stars and galaxies are moving away from Earth. This stretches their light as it travels through space towards us – the further it travels, the more stretched it becomes. The stretching makes visible light look redder – which is known as the redshift. Eventually, if it travelled and redshifted far enough, the light would no longer be visible, and would become first infrared and then microwave radiation (as used on Earth in microwave ovens). This is just what has happened to the incredibly powerful light produced by the Big Bang – after 13 billion years of travelling it is detectable today as microwaves coming from every direction in space. This has the grand title of *Cosmic Microwave Background Radiation*, and is nothing less than the afterglow of the Big Bang itself.

Annie said all this matter of factly, as though it was quite normal to know this kind of information and be able to rattle it off at parties. But once again, George felt a little jealous of her. He loved science and was always reading books, looking up articles on the internet and pestering Annie's scientist father, Eric, with questions. He wanted to be a scientist when he grew up, so he could learn everything there was to know and maybe make some amazing discovery of his own. Annie, on the other hand, was much more casual about the wonders of the Universe.

When George had first met her, she'd wanted to be a ballerina, but now she'd changed her mind and decided on being a footballer. Instead of spending her time after school in a pink and white tutu, she now charged around the back garden hammering a football past George, who was always made to stand in goal. And yet she still seemed to know far more about science than he did.

Annie's dad, Eric, now appeared, dressed in his normal clothes and looking no different from usual.

'Eric,' cried George, who was bursting with questions, 'what have you come as?'

'Oh, me?' Eric smiled. 'I'm the only intelligent life form in the Universe,' he said modestly.

'What?' asked George. 'You mean you're the only intelligent person in the whole Universe?'

Eric laughed. 'Don't say that too loudly round here,'

he told George, gesturing to all the other scientists. 'Otherwise people will get very upset. I meant, I've come as a human being, which is the only intelligent form of life in the Universe that we know about. So far.'

'Oh,' said George. 'But what about all your friends? What have they come as? And why does red light mean something is going away? I don't understand.'

'Well,' said Eric kindly, 'you'd understand if someone explained it to you.'

'Can *you* explain it to me?' pleaded George. 'All about the Universe? Like you did with the black holes? Can you tell me about red thingies and dark matter and everything else?'

'Oh dear,' said Eric, sounding rather regretful. 'George, I'd love to tell you all about the Universe, but the problem is, I'm just not sure I'll have time before I have to . . . Hang on a second . . .' He trailed off and gazed into the distance, the way he did when he was having an idea. He took off his glasses and polished them on his shirt, setting them on his nose at the same wonky angle as before. 'I've got it!' he cried, sounding very excited. 'I know what we need to do! Hold on, George, I've got a clever plan.'

With that, he picked up a soft hammer and struck a huge brass gong, which rang out with a deep, humming chime.

'Right, gather round, everyone,' said Eric, waving everyone into the room. 'Come on, come on, hurry up! I've got something to say.'

A ripple of excitement went through the crowd.

'Now then,' he went on, 'I've gathered the Order of Science here today for this party —'

'Hurray!' cheered someone at the back.

'And I want us to put our minds to some questions my young friend George has asked me. He wants to know all sorts of things! For a start, I'm sure he'll want to know what your costume is!' He pointed to the man wearing the hula hoops.

'I've come to the party,' piped up the cheerful-looking scientist, 'as a distant planetary system where we might find another planet Earth.'

'Annie,' whispered George, 'isn't that what Doctor Reeper did? Find new planets?'

Dr Reeper was a former colleague of Eric's who wanted to use science for his own selfish purposes. He had told Eric he'd found an exoplanet – that is, a planet in orbit around a star other than the Earth's Sun – that might be able to support human life. But the directions he'd given Eric had been bogus – in fact, in his search for the planet, they had sent Eric dangerously close to a black hole. Dr Reeper had been trying to get rid of Eric so he could control Cosmos, Eric's super-computer. But his evil trick hadn't worked and Eric had returned safely from his trip inside a black hole.

No one knew where Dr Reeper was now – he had fled after his masterplan backfired. At the time, George had begged Eric to do something about him, but Eric had just let him go.

'Doctor Reeper knew how to *look* for planets,' said Annie, 'but we don't know whether he ever actually found one. After all, that planet he wrote about in the letter to Dad – we never got to see whether it really existed or not.'

'Thank you, Sam. And how many planets have you found so far?' Eric questioned the hula-hoop man.

'So far,' replied Sam, shivering his hoops as he spoke, 'three hundred and thirty-one exoplanets – over a hundred of them in orbit around stars quite nearby. Some of these stars have more than one planet going around them.' He motioned to his hula-hoop rings. 'I'm a nearby system with planets in orbit around its star.'

'What does he mean by "nearby"?' George whispered to Annie, who passed the message on to Eric. Her father whispered back to her, and she then relayed the answer to George.

'He means, maybe, like, about forty light years away. So, like, about two hundred and thirty-five trillion miles,' said Annie. 'Nearby for the Universe!'

'Have you seen anything that might be like the Earth? A planet we could call home?'

'We've seen a few that might – and only might – be like a second Earth. Our planet-hunting search continues.'

'Thank you, Sam,' said Eric. 'Now, what I want us to do is answer George's questions – all of us. Each of you' – he handed out pens and paper – 'can write me a page or two by the end of the party about what you think is the most interesting part of the science you work on. You can post or email it to me later if you don't have time to finish it now.'

The scientists all looked really happy. They *loved* talking about the most interesting bits of their work.

'And,' added Eric quickly, 'before we get back to the party, I've got one more brief announcement to make – one of my own this time. I'm very excited and pleased to tell you all that I have a new job! I'm going to work for the Global Space Agency, looking for signs of life in our Solar System. Beginning with Mars!'

'Wow!' said George. 'That's amazing!' He turned to Annie but she didn't meet his eye.

'So,' continued Eric, 'in just a few days' time, my family and I will be packing up . . . and moving to the headquarters of the Global Space Agency in the United States of America!'

With that, George's universe imploded.

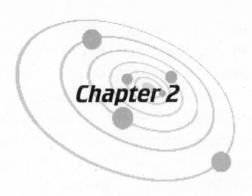

Chapter 2

George hated watching his next-door neighbours pack up their house and get ready to leave. But he wanted to spend as much time with them as he could before they vanished from his life. So day after day, he went round there and saw how the house got bigger

and bigger inside, as more and more of their things were swallowed up, first by big cardboard boxes marked with Global Space Agency stickers and then by the vans that kept arriving to take them all away.

'It's so exciting!' Annie kept exclaiming. 'We're going to America! We're going to be movie stars! We're going to eat huge burgers! We're going to see New York! We're going . . .' On and on she went about her fabulous new life and how much better everything would be when she was living in a different country. Sometimes George tried to suggest that maybe it

wouldn't be quite as amazing as she thought. But Annie was too carried away by her fantasy life in the USA to pay him much attention.

Eric and Susan tried a bit harder to mask their excitement at the big move so as not to hurt George's feelings. But even they couldn't hide it from him entirely. One day, when the house was nearly empty, George sat in Eric's library, helping him wrap his precious scientific objects in old newspaper and put them carefully into big boxes.

'You'll come back, won't you?' pleaded George. All the pictures had come off the walls now and the shelves were nearly bare of the books that had lined the room. The house was starting to feel as empty and desolate as it had when they'd first moved in.

'That depends!' said Eric cheerfully. 'Maybe I'll hitch a lift on the next mission into space and go out there for ever.' He caught sight of George's desolate face. 'No, no, I don't mean that,' he added hastily. 'I couldn't leave you all behind. I'd make sure I had a way back to planet Earth.'

'But will you come back and live here?' persisted George. 'In your house?'

'It's not really my house,' said Eric. 'It's just a place I was given to go, where I could work on Cosmos without anyone finding out. But unfortunately, someone – or rather Graham Reeper – was here already, lying in wait for me.'

'How did Doctor Reeper know that you'd come here?' asked George, wrapping up an old telescope.

'Ah, well, looking back, of course I realize this place was a far more obvious choice than I realized,' replied Eric. 'You see, this house belonged to our former tutor, one of the greatest scientists that ever lived. No one knows where he is right now – he seems to have disappeared. But before that happened he wrote me a letter, offering me this house as a safe place to work with Cosmos. It was so important to keep Cosmos away from harm, but in the end, I just couldn't do that.' He looked really sad.

George put down the telescope and reached for his school satchel. He got out a packet of Jammy Dodgers, ripped them open and passed them over. Eric smiled at the sight of his favourite biscuits. 'I should really make us a cup of tea to go with your biscuits,' he said. 'But I think I've packed the kettle.'

George crunched the Jammy Dodger between his teeth. 'What I don't understand,' he said, realizing this might be his last chance to ask, 'is why you don't just build another Cosmos.'

'If I could,' said Eric, 'I would. But my tutor, Graham Reeper and I built the prototype of Cosmos together, many years ago. The modern version of Cosmos still has some of the original features from that first computer. That's why it's not possible for me to simply build another one. Without the other two, I'm not sure I know how. One of them has vanished and the other, Reeper – well, we know all about him. In a way' – Eric licked the jam out of the centre of the biscuit – 'Cosmos breaking down has changed all our lives. Now I don't have him, I have to look for other ways to continue my work in space. And it means I'm not always worrying that someone will find out about my super-computer and try to steal him. We moved so many times, in order to keep Cosmos out of danger. Poor Annie, she's lived in so many different houses. But this is the one where she's been happiest.'

'You wouldn't know it,' said George darkly. 'She doesn't seem sad to be going.'

'She doesn't want to leave you – you're her best friend,' Eric told him. 'She's going to miss you, George, even if she doesn't show it. She won't find another friend like you in a hurry.'

George gulped. 'I'll miss her too,' he muttered, turning bright red. 'And you. And Susan.'

'We'll see each other again,' said Eric gently. 'You won't be missing us for ever. And if you ever need me, you know that you just have to let me know. I'll do anything I can for you, George.'

'Um, thanks,' muttered George. A thought struck him. 'But is it safe for you to go?' he said, clutching at a ray of hope. 'Shouldn't you stay here? What if Reeper follows you to the USA?'

'I don't think there's much poor old Reeper can do to me now,' said Eric sadly.

'Poor old Reeper?' exclaimed George hotly.

'He tried to throw you into a black hole! I don't understand why you feel sorry for him! I don't get it – why didn't you do something about him when you had the chance?'

'I've ruined enough of Reeper's life already,' said Eric. George opened his mouth to speak but Eric cut him off. 'Look, George,' he said firmly, 'Reeper's had a jolly good go at me already and I expect that's enough for him. He's had his revenge and I don't think I'll be hearing from him again. Anyway, Cosmos doesn't work any more so I don't have anything that Reeper would want. I'm safe, my family is safe, and now I want to go to the Global Space Agency. They've offered me the chance to work on finding signs of life on Mars and in other places in the Solar System. You do understand I couldn't refuse?'

'S'pose so,' said George. 'Will you tell me if you find anyone out there in space?'

'I most certainly will,' promised Eric. 'You'll be among the first to know. And, George . . . I want you to keep this telescope.' He pointed to the bronze cylinder that George had been carefully wrapping in paper. 'It's to remind you to keep looking at the stars.'

'Really?' said George in wonder, unwrapping the telescope again and feeling the cool smooth metal under his hand. 'But isn't it very valuable?'

'Well, so are you. And so are the observations you'll make when you use it. To help you, I've got another special leaving present for you.' Eric dived into a nearby pile of books and finally, triumphantly, came up with a bright yellow volume, which he waved in the air at George. On the front in big letters it said:

The User's Guide to the Universe.

'Do you remember,' he asked George, 'when I asked all my science friends at the party to write a page for me, answering some of the questions you posed? Well, I made their answers into a book – one for you and one for Annie. Here it is! When you read it, remember that I wanted you to understand something about being a scientist. I wanted to show you that me and my friends – we call each other colleagues – love to read each other's work and talk about it. We exchange our theories and our ideas, and that's one of the really important – and fun – parts of being a scientist: having colleagues who help, inspire and challenge you. That's what this book is all about. I thought maybe you'd like to look at the first few pages with me. I wrote them myself,' he added modestly.

Eric started to read:

WHY DO WE GO INTO SPACE?

Why do we go into space? Why go to all that effort and spend all that money just for a few lumps of Moon rock? Aren't there better things we could be doing here on Earth?

Well, it's a bit like Europe before 1492. Back then, people thought it was a big waste of money to send Christopher Columbus off on a wild goose chase. But then he discovered America and that made a huge difference. Just think – if he hadn't, we wouldn't have the Big Mac. And lots of other things, of course.

Spreading out into space will have an even greater effect. It will completely change the future of the human race; it could decide whether we have a future at all.

It won't solve any of our immediate problems on planet Earth, but it will help us look at them in a different way. The time has come when we need to look outwards across the Universe rather than inwards at ourselves on an increasingly over-crowded planet.

Moving the human race out into space won't happen quickly. By that, I mean it could take hundreds, or even thousands, of years. We could have a base on the Moon within thirty years, reach Mars in fifty years, and explore the moons of the outer planets in 200 years. By reach, I mean with manned – or should I say *personed*? – flight. We have already driven rovers on Mars and landed a probe on Titan, a moon of Saturn, but when we're dealing with the future of the human race, we have to go there ourselves and not just send robots.

But go where? Now that astronauts have lived for months on the International Space Station, we know that human beings can survive away from planet Earth. But we also know that living in zero gravity on the Space Station doesn't just make it difficult to have a cup of tea! It's not very good for people to live in zero gravity for a long time, so if we're to have a base in space we need it to be on a planet or moon.

So which one shall we choose? The most obvious is the Moon. It is close, and quite easy to get to. We've already landed on it, and driven across it in a buggy. On the other hand, the Moon is small, and without an atmosphere or a magnetic field to deflect the solar wind particles, like on Earth. There is no liquid water, but there may be ice in the craters at the north and south poles. A colony on the Moon could use this as a source of oxygen, with power provided by nuclear energy or solar panels. The Moon could be a base for travel to the rest of the Solar System.

What about Mars? That's our next obvious target. Mars is further from the Sun than planet Earth is, so it gets less warmth from the sunlight, making temperatures much colder. Once, Mars had a magnetic field, but that decayed four billion years ago, meaning that it was stripped of most of its atmosphere, leaving it with only one per cent of the pressure of the Earth's atmosphere.

In the past, the atmospheric pressure – which means the weight of the air above you in the atmosphere – must have been higher because we can see what appear to be dried-up channels and lakes. Liquid water cannot exist on Mars now as it would just evaporate.

However, there is lots of water in the form of ice at the two poles. If we went to live on Mars, we could use this. We could also use the minerals and metals that volcanoes have brought to the surface.

So the Moon and Mars might be quite good for us. But where else could we go in the Solar System? Mercury and Venus are way too hot, while Jupiter and Saturn are gas giants, with no solid surface.

We could try the moons of Mars but they are very small. Some of the moons of Jupiter and Saturn might be better. Titan, a moon of Saturn, is larger and more massive than our Moon, and has a dense atmosphere. The Cassini-Huygens mission of NASA and ESA, the European Space Agency, has landed a probe on Titan, which sent back pictures of the surface. However, it is very cold, being so far from the Sun, and I wouldn't fancy living next to a lake of liquid methane.

What about beyond our Solar System? From looking across the Universe, we know that quite a few stars have planets in orbit around them. Until recently we could see only giant planets the size of Jupiter or Saturn. But now we are starting to spot smaller Earth-like planets too. Some of these will lie in the Goldilocks Zone, where their distance from the home star is in the right range for liquid water to exist on their surface. There are maybe a thousand stars within ten light years of Earth. If one per cent of these have an Earth-sized planet in the Goldilocks Zone, we have ten candidate new worlds.

At the moment we can't travel very far across the Universe. In fact, we can't even imagine how we might be able to cover such huge distances. But that's what we should be aiming to do in the future, over the next 200 to 500 years. The human race has existed as a separate species for about two million years. Civilization began about 10,000 years ago, and the rate of development has been steadily increasing. We have now reached the stage where we can boldly go where no one has gone before. And who knows what we will find and who we will meet?

Good luck on all your cosmic journeys, and I hope you find our little book useful.

Inter-stellar best wishes,

Eric

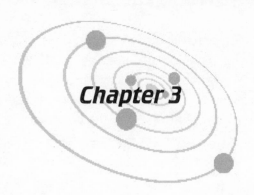

Chapter 3

Finally, the day came when the doors slammed on the last vanload of Eric, Annie and Susan's belongings and they were standing in the street, saying goodbye to George and his parents.

'Don't worry!' said George's dad. 'I'll keep an eye on the house for you. Might tidy up the garden a bit.' He gave Eric a firm handshake, which made the scientist turn rather pale and rub his hand afterwards.

George's mum hugged Annie. 'Who's going to kick a football over my fence now?' she said. 'My vegetable patch is going to find life very quiet.'

Annie whispered something in her ear. Daisy smiled. 'Of course you can.' She turned to George. 'Annie would like to say goodbye to Freddy,' she told him.

George nodded, not wanting to speak in case his voice wobbled. In silence, the two of them went through George's house and out into the back garden.

'Goodbye, Freddy,' cooed Annie, leaning over the pigsty. 'I'm going to miss you so much!'

George took a deep breath. 'Freddy's going to miss you too,' he said, his voice squeaking a bit from the effort of holding back the tears. 'He really likes you,' he added. 'He's had a really great time since you've been here – it isn't going to be the same once you're gone.'

'I've had a great time as well,' said Annie sadly.

'Freddy hopes you don't find another pig in America that you like as much as him,' said George.

'I'll *never* like another pig as much as Freddy,' declared Annie. 'He's my best pig ever!'

'Annie!' they heard Susan calling through the house. 'Annie, we have to go!'

'Freddy thinks you're ace,' said George. 'And he'll be waiting for you when you get back.'

'Bye, George,' said Annie.

'Bye, Annie,' said George. 'See you in space.'

Annie walked slowly away. George climbed into the pigsty and sat on the warm straw. 'It's just you and me now, Freddy, my cosmic pig,' he said sadly. 'Just like it was before.'

After Eric, Susan and Annie had left, it seemed horribly quiet in the back garden. The days stretched on and on, each one pretty much the same as the last. There was nothing particularly wrong with George's life these days – the horrible Dr Reeper had left the school, and now that George had won the big science competition, he had found some friends to spend his lunch breaks with. The bullies – who had given him such a hard time when Dr Reeper was around – tended to leave him alone these days. At home, George had his computer so he could find out interesting stuff for his homework – or about science in general, in which he was more and more interested – and send emails to his friends. He regularly logged on to the various space sites to read about all the new discoveries. He loved looking at the pictures taken by space-based observatories like the Hubble Space Telescope and reading accounts of space journeys by astronauts.

But although this was all really fascinating, it wasn't the same without Annie and her family to share these discoveries with. Each night, George looked up into the sky in the hope of seeing a shooting star fall towards Earth, as a sign that his cosmic adventures were not yet over. But one never came.

Then one day, just as he had given up hope, he got a very surprising email from Annie. He'd written to her lots of times, and in return received rambling messages full of long boring stories about kids he'd never met.

But this message was different. It read:

George, Mum and Dad have written to your parents to ask you to come and stay in the holidays. YOU MUST COME! Le fact is, I need you. Have COSMIC mission! Do not chicken out!!
Elderly loons are useless, so say nothing of space adventures to them. Even Dad says NO, which is situation serious. So pretend is normal holiday. SPACESUITS AT THE READY! YRS IN THE UNIVERSE, Axxx.

George emailed her straight back:

What?? When?? Where??

But her reply was short:

Can say no more for now. Make plans to come. Raid bank for ticket and get here, Axx.

George just sat there, staring at the screen in shock. There was nothing he wanted more than to go and see Annie and her family in Florida, USA. He would go like a shot even if there wasn't an adventure in the offing. But how? How would he get there? What if his parents said no? Would he have to run away from home and hide on an ocean liner to get there? Or sneak onto an aeroplane when no one was looking? He'd slipped out into space through a computer-generated portal when he wasn't supposed to. But getting to America suddenly seemed far more complicated than fishing someone out of a black hole. Life on Earth . . . he thought to himself. Much trickier than life in space.

Then he had a good idea. *Gran*, he thought to himself. *That's who I need*. He emailed her.

> Dear Gran. Must go to America. Have been invited to stay with a friend but need to go SOON! Is very very important. Sorry can't explain. Can you help me?

The answer pinged back in just a few seconds:

> On my way over, George. Sit tight, all will be well. Love Gran xx

Sure enough, just an hour later, there was a ferocious banging on the front door. George's dad went to open it, but as soon as he did so, he was barged out of the way by his mother, who was waving a cane and looking very cross.

'Terence, George must go to America to stay with his friends,' she announced, without so much as a hello. She brandished her walking stick at George's dad.

'Mother,' he said, looking furious, 'how dare you interfere?'

'I can't hear you – I'm deaf, you know,' she said, thrusting a notebook and pen at him.

'Mother, I am very well aware of that,' he said through gritted teeth.

'You'll have to write it down!' said Gran. 'I can't hear you! I can't hear a word you say.'

George going to Florida – or not – is none of your business, he wrote in her notepad.

Gran looked over at George and winked craftily at him. He flashed a quick smile back.

George's mum had come in from the garden and was wiping her muddy hands on a towel. 'That's very odd, George,' she said quietly, 'because only this morning we opened a letter from Susan and Eric, inviting you to stay for the school holidays. How does your gran know about this already?'

'Um, perhaps Gran is psychic?' said George quickly.

'I see,' said his mum, giving him a funny look. 'The thing is, George, Eric and Susan told me they were asking us first, before you knew about the invitation, in case it wasn't possible for you to come. They didn't want you to be disappointed if it didn't work out. And, you see, we just can't afford the fare, George.'

'Then I'll pay for him to go,' retorted Gran.

'Oh, you heard that, did you?' said George's dad, who was still scribbling away in the notebook.

'I lip-read,' said Gran hastily. 'I can't hear a thing. I'm deaf, you know!'

You can't afford to send George to America! George's mum wrote in her notepad.

'Don't you tell me what I can and can't do!' said Gran. 'I've got pots of money, all hidden under the floorboards. More than I know how to spend. And if you silly people won't let him go by himself, then I'll fly out with him – I've got some friends in Florida whom I haven't seen in years.' She grinned at George again. 'What do you say, George?' she asked.

With a huge smile on his face, George nodded at her so many times, his head looked like it might fall off. But then he turned to his parents to see how they were taking it. He couldn't believe they would agree to any of this, especially as it meant travelling on an aeroplane – something his mum and dad didn't approve of, in theory.

But Gran had thought of that problem already. 'You know,' she said airily, 'I don't see why it should be just George and I who get to go away. After all, Terence, you and Daisy haven't been anywhere exciting for a very long time. There must be somewhere you'd like to go – somewhere in the world you could do some good; somewhere you could really make a difference, if only you had the time and the air ticket to get there.'

George's dad gasped and George realized that clever Gran had spoken right to his heart.

'Isn't there something you'd love to do?' she persisted.

Her son wasn't looking angry any more but hopeful instead. 'You know,' he said to George's mum, '*if* George did go to Florida for the summer holidays and Mother would help us out with the air fares, it would mean that we could go on that other trip ourselves – the eco-mission to the South Pacific.'

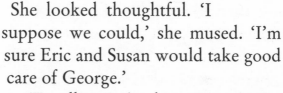

She looked thoughtful. 'I suppose we could,' she mused. 'I'm sure Eric and Susan would take good care of George.'

'Excellent!' piped up Gran, intent on closing the deal before anyone could change their minds. 'It's a plan. George goes to Florida and you can have a holiday – I mean, save the world,' she corrected herself quickly. 'I'll buy the tickets for everyone and we'll be off.'

George's dad shook his head at his mother. 'Sometimes I think you only hear what you want to hear.'

Gran just smiled regretfully and pointed to her ears. 'Didn't catch that,' she said firmly. 'Not a word.'

George felt the laughter bubbling up inside him. Because of Gran, he might be going to America! Where Annie was waiting for him with some hot news about her discovery. He felt a bit guilty about his mum and dad. They thought they were sending him off for a nice, safe, quiet vacation in a different country. But George knew enough about Annie's way of working to suspect it was going to be anything but safe and quiet. And she'd mentioned the spacesuits in her message – the ones they'd worn to fly around the Solar System. It must mean she had uncovered a secret that had to do with space and she wanted him to travel out there with her once more. He held his breath while he waited for his mum to speak.

'All right then,' she said, after the longest pause. 'If Gran is offering to take you to Florida and Eric and Susan will meet you the minute your plane touches down and take care of you the whole time, I suppose I have to say *yes*!'

'YES!' said George, punching the air. 'Thanks, Mum, thanks, Dad, thanks, Gran. Better go pack!' With that, like a little whirlwind, he was gone.

* * *

It was so exciting to be packing up himself to go on a journey rather than watching other people fill their suitcases. George had no idea what to take with him so he just threw things around his room for a while and made an incredible mess.

He didn't know much about America – just what he'd seen on TV shows when he'd been at friends' houses. That didn't give him much of a clue to what he might need in Florida. A skateboard? Some cool clothes? He didn't have either. He packed some of his books and clothes and put his precious copy of *The User's Guide to the Universe* in his school bag, which he was using as his carry-on luggage for the plane. As for packing for a trip into space, George knew that astronauts only took a change of clothes and some chocolate with them, but then they went up in spaceships and he doubted even Annie had managed to arrange one of them.

As George got ready to leave, so did his parents. They had decided to go on the eco-mission while he was on holiday. They were going to join a ship in the South Pacific that was helping some islanders whose lives were being threatened by rising sea water.

'We'll be in touch as often as we can from the sinking islands – by email or phone,' George's dad told him. 'Find out how you're getting on. Eric and Susan have promised to look after you. And Gran' – he sighed – 'will be nearby, if you need her.' Even Freddy the pig got to take a holiday – he was going to spend the summer at a local children's farm.

George couldn't sleep at all the night before the flight. He was off to the USA to see his best friend and maybe, just maybe, go out into space again. He'd flown around the Solar System before but he'd never actually been on an aeroplane, so that was exciting too. Before, he'd been far away in outer space, but this time he would be flying through the Earth's atmosphere. He would be travelling through the part where the sky is still blue, before it turns to the black of space.

On the plane, he looked out of the window at the white fluffy clouds below. Above them, he could see the Sun, the star at the centre of our Solar System, radiating down heat and energy. Below was his planet, which he saw in snatches when the clouds parted.

Gran slept for most of the journey, giving out tiny gentle whooshes of air, just like Freddy did when he was dozing. While she slept, George got out his *User's Guide to the Universe* and read about another voyage – this one not just across our planet but across our whole Universe.

A VOYAGE ACROSS THE UNIVERSE

We will now go on a voyage across the Universe.

Before setting out we must understand what we mean by the terms 'voyage' and 'Universe'. The word 'Universe' literally means everything that exists. However, the history of astronomy might be regarded as a sequence of steps, at each of which the Universe has appeared to get bigger. So what we mean by 'everything' has changed.

Nowadays most cosmologists accept the Big Bang theory – according to which the Universe started in a state of great compression around 14 billion years ago. This means that the furthest we can see is the distance that light has travelled since the Big Bang. This defines the size of the *observable* Universe.

So what is meant by a 'voyage'? First we must distinguish between *peering* across the Universe and *travelling* across it. *Peering* is what astronomers do and, as we will see, involves looking back in time. Travelling is what astronauts do and involves crossing space. This also involves another kind of voyage. For as we travel from the Earth to the edge of the observable Universe, we are essentially retracing the history of human thought about the scale of the Universe. We will now discuss these three journeys in turn.

The voyage back through time

The information astronomers receive comes from electromagnetic waves that travel at the speed of light (186,000 miles per second). This is very fast but it is finite and astronomers often measure distance by the equivalent light travel time. Light takes several minutes to reach us from the Sun, for instance, but years from the nearest star, millions of years from the nearest big galaxy (Andromeda) and many billions of years from the most distant galaxies.

This means that as one peers across greater *distances*, one is also looking further into the *past*. For example, if we observe a galaxy 10 million light-years *away*, we are seeing it as it was 10 million years *ago*. A voyage across the Universe in this sense is therefore not only a journey through *space*; it is also a journey back through *time* – right back to the Big Bang itself.

We cannot actually observe all the way back to the Big Bang. The early Universe was so hot that it formed a fog of particles that we cannot see through. As the Universe expanded, it cooled and the fog lifted about 400,000 years after the Big Bang. However, we can still use our theories to speculate what the Universe was like before then. Since the density and temperature increase as we go back in time, our speculation depends on our theories of high energy physics, but we now have a fairly complete picture of the history of the Universe.

One might expect that our voyage back through time would end at the Big Bang. However, scientists are now trying to understand the physics of creation itself and any mechanism that can produce our Universe could in principle generate others. For example, some people believe the Universe undergoes cycles of expansion and re-collapse, giving us universes strung out in time. Others think that our Universe is just one of many 'bubbles' spread out in space. These are variants of what is called the 'multiverse' proposal.

The voyage across space

Travelling across the Universe physically is much more challenging because of the time it would take. Einstein's Special Theory of Relativity (1905) suggests that no spaceship could travel faster than the speed of light. This means it would take at least 100,000 years to cross the Galaxy and 10 billion years to cross the Universe – at least as judged by someone who stays on Earth. But Special Relativity also predicts that time flows more slowly for moving observers, so the trip could be much quicker for the astronauts themselves. Indeed, if one could travel at the speed of light, no time at all would pass!

No spaceship can travel as fast as light, but one could still gradually accelerate towards this maximum speed; the time experienced would then be much shorter than that on Earth. For example, if one were propelled with the acceleration with which bodies fall due to gravity on Earth, a journey across the Galaxy would only seem to take about 30 years. One could therefore return to Earth in one's *own* lifetime, although one's friends would have died long ago. If one continued to accelerate beyond the Galaxy for a century, one could, in principle, travel to the edge of the currently observable Universe!

Einstein's General Theory of Relativity (1915) could allow even more exotic possibilities. For example, maybe astronauts could one day use wormholes or spacewarp effects – just like in *Star Trek* and other popular science fiction series – to make these journeys even faster and get home again without losing any friends. But this is all very speculative.

The voyage through the history of human thought

To the ancient Greeks, the Earth was the centre of the Universe, with the planets, the Sun and the stars being relatively close. This *geocentric* view (Earth = *geos*) was demolished in the sixteenth century, when Copernicus showed that the Earth and other planets move around the Sun (*helios*). However, this *heliocentric* picture did not last very long. Several decades later, Galileo used his newly invented telescope to show that the Milky Way – then known only as a band of light in the sky – consists of numerous stars like the Sun. This discovery not only diminished the status of the Sun, it also vastly increased the size of the known Universe.

By the eighteenth century it was accepted that the Milky Way is a disc of stars (the Galaxy), held together by gravity. However, most astronomers still assumed that the Milky Way comprised the whole Universe and this *galacto-centric* view persisted well into the twentieth century. Then, in 1924, Edwin Hubble measured the distance to our nearest neighbouring galaxy (Andromeda) and showed that it had to be well outside the Milky Way. Another shift in the size of the Universe!

Within a few more years Hubble had obtained data on several dozen nearby galaxies, which showed that they are all moving away from us at a speed that is proportional to their distance from us. The easiest way to picture this is to think of space itself as expanding, just like the surface of an inflating balloon onto which the galaxies are painted. This expansion is known as Hubble's Law, and it has now been shown to apply up to distances of tens of billions of light-years, a region containing hundreds of billions of galaxies. Yet another huge shift of scale!

The *cosmocentric* view regards this as the final shift in the size of the Universe. This is because the cosmic expansion means that, as one goes back in time, the galaxies get closer together and eventually merge. Before that, the density just continues to increase – back to the 'Big Bang' 14 billion years ago – and we can never see *beyond* the distance travelled by light since then. However, recently there has been an interesting observational development. Although one expects the expansion of the Universe to slow down because of gravity, current observations suggest that it is actually *accelerating*. Theories to explain this suggest that our observable universe could be a part of a much larger 'bubble'. And this bubble could itself be just one of many bubbles, as in the multiverse proposal!

What next?

So the endpoint of all three of our journeys – the first back through time, the second across space, and the third retracing the history of human thought – is the same: those unobservable universes which can only be glimpsed through theories and visited in our minds!

I wonder what tomorrow's astronomers will discover . . .

When the plane landed, George and Gran joined the queue to get through immigration and customs. Eric and Annie were waiting in the arrivals area. Annie shrieked and jumped up and down on the other side of the barrier as soon as she saw him.

'George!' she hollered. 'George!' She ducked under the rail and grabbed him. She was taller and browner than he remembered. She hugged him and whispered in his ear, 'It is sooooo good you are here! Can't tell you now but we are in an emergency! But remember, shush!

Say nothing.' She took his trolley and careered off with it towards Eric. Gran and George hurried after her.

George had a shock when he saw Eric. He looked so tired, with some strands of white in his dark hair. But he smiled when he saw George, and his face lit up just like it used to.

They said their hellos and Gran shook hands with Eric and got him to write down comments in her note-book. Then she gave him an envelope marked *George's Emergency Fund*, hugged her grandson, grinned at

Annie and went off to greet her friends, who had come to the airport to meet her. 'A bunch of old rogues and rebels from my past who live near Eric and Susan,' she had told George. 'Nice chance for us to relive some of our high jinks.'

But the people who came to collect Gran were so old and wobbly-looking George couldn't imagine them ever being young, let alone having an adventure. She tottered off into the distance with them and he felt his stomach shrink as he watched her leave. It seemed very big and bright here in America – everything was much shinier and larger and louder than it was at home. A wave of homesickness struck him. But not for long.

A smaller boy with thick glasses and a very peculiar hairstyle had appeared from behind Eric.

'Greetings, George,' he said earnestly. 'Annie' – he shot her a look of total disgust – 'has told me all about you. I have been eagerly anticipating interfacing with you. You sound a most interesting person.'

'Back off, Emmett,' said Annie fiercely. 'George is *my* friend and he's come to see *me*, not you.'

'George, this is Emmett,' Eric told him calmly while Annie glared at Emmett and Emmett looked away with pursed lips. 'He is the son of one of my friends. Emmett is staying with us for a while this summer.'

'He's the son of doom, more likely,' Annie whispered in George's ear.

Emmett snuck around to George's other side and hissed in his other ear, 'The girl humanoid is a total moron.'

'As maybe you can tell,' continued Eric lightly, 'there's been a small falling out between these two.'

'I told him not to touch my Girl's World action doll!' Annie exploded. 'And now it only speaks Klingon.'

'I didn't ask her to cut my hair,' Emmett bleated. 'And now I look stupid.'

'You looked stupid before,' muttered Annie.

'Better speaking Klingon than just garbage like you,' retorted Emmett. His big eyes, magnified by his glasses, looked very shiny.

'George has had a long journey,' said Eric firmly. 'So we are going to take him to the car and drive home and everyone is going to be nice to everyone else. Do you hear me?' He sounded quite stern.

'Yes!' said George.

'It's all right, George,' said Eric. 'You're always nice. It's the others I'm worried about.'

Chapter 4

Eric drove them to the big white wooden house where his family now lived. The sun was beating down from the perfectly blue sky and the heat rose up from the ground to smack George in the face as he got out of the car. Annie scrambled out after him. 'Come on,' she said as Eric unloaded George's bag from the boot. 'We've got work to do. Follow me.' She took him round to the back of the house, where a huge tree shaded a veranda with a table and chairs on it.

'Up the tree!' Annie instructed him. 'It's the only place we can talk!' She shinned up to a large over-hanging branch. George slowly clambered after her. Susan had come out onto the veranda, carrying a tray. She stood underneath Annie and George, with Emmett close behind her.

'Hello, George!' she called up into the tree. 'It's nice to see you! Even if I can't actually see you.'

'Hello, Susan,' George called back. 'Thanks for inviting me.'

'Annie, don't you think George might like a rest?

And something to eat and drink after his journey?'

'Give it to the tree,' said Annie, sticking her head out through the papery green and white leaves. She reached down with an arm and grabbed a juice box, which she handed back to George, and then a load of cookies.

'OK, we're good now!' she sang. 'Bye, other people! You can vamoose!'

Emmett just stood there, looking longingly up into the tree.

'Can Emmett come up and join you?' asked Susan.

'Quite literally,' said Annie, 'no. He might fall out

of one of the brancheroonies and damage his amazing brain cell count. Better stay safely on the ground. Ciao, you guys! George and I are busy.'

From the tree, they heard Susan sigh. 'Why don't you sit here?' she said to Emmett, arranging a chair for him under the branches. 'I'm sure they'll come down soon.'

Emmett made a small snuffling noise and they heard Susan comforting him.

'Ignore him – he's a total crybaby!' Annie whispered to George. 'And don't start feeling sorry for him – that's lethal. The minute you show weakness, he pounces. I felt sorry for him the first time he cried. And then he bit me. My mum's too soppy – she just can't see it.'

Susan's footsteps tapped away into the house.

'Right, hold onto that branch,' ordered Annie, 'in case you faint away in shock at what I have to tell you.'

'What is it?' said George.

'Huge news,' confirmed Annie. 'So huge-ously huge your bottom will fall through your pants in surprise.' She looked at him expectantly.

'Well, tell me,' said George patiently.

'Promise you won't think I've gone bananas?'

'Um, well, I pretty much thought you were already,' admitted George. 'So that won't change anything.'

Annie swatted him with her free hand.

'Ouch!' he said, laughing. 'That hurt.'

'George, are you OK?' came a little voice from below. 'Do you need protection from the renegade one? She can be really evil.'

'Shut up, Emmett,' Annie shouted down. 'And stop listening to our conversation.'

'I'm not trying to listen!' came Emmett's high-pitched whine. 'It's not my fault that you're sending a stream of useless vibrations into the atmosphere.'

'Then go somewhere else!' yelled Annie.

'No!' said Emmett obstinately. 'I'm staying here in case George needs my super-intelligent assistance. I don't want him to waste his bandwidth on your rudimentary communication.'

Annie rolled her eyes up to heaven and sighed. She inched along the branch towards George and whispered in his ear:

'I've had a message from aliens.'

'Aliens!' said George loudly, forgetting about Emmett below. 'You've had a message from aliens!'

'Shush!' said Annie frantically. But it was too late.

'Does the young female humanoid really believe that a life form intelligent enough to send a message across the vast expanse of space would pick her to receive it?' said Emmett, standing up and looking into the tree. 'And anyway, there are no aliens. We have no proof of another intelligent life form in the Universe at this moment. We can only calculate the probability that on some other planets there are conditions suitable for forms of extremophile bacteria. Which would have the approximate IQ level of Annie herself. Or probably a bit more. I can calculate the probability of intelligent life for you, if you like, using the Drake Equation.'

THE DRAKE EQUATION

The Drake Equation isn't really an equation; it's a series of questions which help us to work out how many intelligent civilizations with the ability to communicate there might be in our galaxy. It was formulated in 1961 by Dr Frank Drake of the SETI Institute, and is still used by scientists today.

This is the Drake Equation:

$$N = N^* \times f_p \times n_e \times f_l \times f_i \times f_c \times L$$

N^* represents the number of new stars born each year in the Milky Way Galaxy

Question: What is the birth rate of stars in the Milky Way Galaxy?
Answer: Our Galaxy is about 12 billion years old, and contains roughly 300 billion stars. So, on average, stars are born at a rate of 300 billion divided by 12 billion = 25 stars per year.

f_p is the fraction of those stars that have planets around them

Question: What percentage of stars have planetary systems?
Answer: Current estimates range from 20% to 70%.

n_e is the number of planets per star that are capable of sustaining life

Question: For each star that does have a planetary system, how many planets are capable of sustaining life?
Answer: Current estimates range from 0.5 to 5.

f_l is the fraction of planets in n_e where life evolves

Question: On what percentage of the planets that are capable of sustaining life does life actually evolve?
Answer: Current estimates range from 100% (where life can evolve, it will) down to close to 0%.

f_i is the fraction of habitable planets with life where intelligent life evolves.

- -

Question: On the planets where life does evolve, what percentage evolves intelligent life?

Answer: Estimates range from 100% (intelligence has such a survival advantage that it will certainly evolve) down to near 0%.

f_c is the fraction of planets with intelligent life capable of interstellar communication

- -

Question: What percentage of intelligent races have the means and the desire to communicate?

Answer: 10% to 20%.

L is the average number of years that a communicating civilization continues to communicate

- -

Question: How long do communicating civilizations last?

Answer: This is the toughest of the questions. If we take Earth as an example, we've been communicating with radio waves for less than 100 years. How long will our civilization continue to communicate with this method? Could we destroy ourselves in a few years, or will we overcome our problems and survive for 10,000 years or more?

When all of these variables are multiplied together we come up with:

N, the number of communicating civilizations in the galaxy.

'Well, thanks for that, Professor Emmett,' said Annie. 'Your Nobel Prize is in the post. So now, why don't you bacteria off yourself? Go find some of your own species to hang out with? Actually, George, there *are* aliens on Earth and Emmett is one of them.'

'No, no, rewind,' said George urgently. 'You've had a message from some aliens? Where? How? What did it say?'

'They sent her a text to say they would be beaming her up to the mother ship at twenty-one hundred hours,' said Emmett. 'We live in hope.'

'Shut up, Emmett.' This time it was George's turn to feel annoyed. 'I want to hear what Annie has to say.'

'OK, here's the scoop!' said Annie. 'Settle down, friends and aliens, and prepare to be amazed.'

Underneath, Emmett was hugging the tree in an attempt to get nearer to them.

George smiled. 'I'm prepared, agent Annie,' he said. 'Go for it.'

'My amazing story,' began Annie, 'starts one ordinary evening when no one could have predicted that for the first time ever in the history of this planet we would finally hear from ET.

'Me, my family and I—' she continued grandly.

'And me!' squeaked Emmett from below.

'And him,' she added, 'had just come back from watching a robot land on Mars. Just your everyday family outing. Nothing special. Except that . . .'

* * *

A few weeks back, Eric, Susan, Annie and Emmett had gone to the Global Space Agency to watch a new type of robot attempt to land on the red planet. The robot, Homer, had taken nine months to travel the 423 million miles to Mars. He was the latest in a series of robots sent by the Agency to explore the planet.

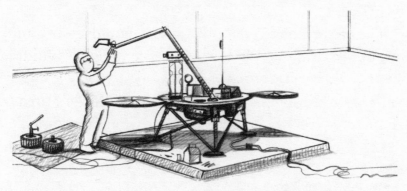

Eric was very excited about Homer touching down on Mars because he had special equipment on board that would help him find out whether there had ever been any life on our nearest neighbour. Homer would be looking for water on Mars: using a special scoop at the end of his long robotic arm, he would scrabble through the icy surface of Mars to pick up handfuls of mud, which he would then bake in a special oven. As Homer heated up the samples of soil, he would be able to discover whether Mars, now a cold desert planet, had once, in its distant, warmer, wetter past, been flowing with water.

ROBOTIC SPACE TRAVEL

A space probe is a robotic spacecraft that scientists send out on a journey across the Solar System in order to gather more information about our cosmic neighbourhood. Robotic space missions aim to answer specific questions such as: 'What does the surface of Venus look like?' 'Is it windy on Neptune?' 'What is Jupiter made of?'

While robotic space missions are much less glamorous than manned space flight, they have several big advantages:

Robots can travel for great distances, going far farther and faster than any astronaut. Like manned missions, they need a source of power – most use solar arrays which convert sunlight to energy, but others which are travelling long distances away from the Sun take their own on-board generator. However, robotic spacecraft need far less power than a manned mission as they don't need to maintain a comfortable living environment on their journey.

Robots also don't need supplies of food or water and they don't need oxygen to breathe, making them much smaller and lighter than a manned spacecraft.

Robots don't get bored or homesick or fall ill on their journey.

If something goes wrong with a robotic mission, no lives are lost in space.

Space probes cost far less than manned space flights and robots don't want to come home when their mission ends.

Space probes have opened up the wonders of the Solar System to us, sending back data which has allowed scientists to understand far better how the Solar System was formed and what conditions are like on other planets. While human beings have to date travelled only as far as the Moon – a journey averaging 378,000 kilometres (235,000 miles), space probes have covered billions of miles and shown us extraordinary and detailed images of the far reaches of the Solar System.

In fact, almost 30 space probes reached the Moon before mankind did! Robotic spacecraft have now been sent to all the other planets in our Solar System, they have caught the

dust from a comet's tail, landed on Mars and Venus and travelled out beyond Pluto. Some space probes have even taken information about our planet and the human race with them. Probes Pioneer 10 and 11 carry engraved plaques with the image of a man and a woman on them and also a map, showing where the probe came from. As the Pioneers journey onward into deep space, they may one day encounter an alien civilization!

The Voyager probes took photographs of cities, landscapes and people on Earth with them as well as a recorded greeting in many different Earth languages. In the incredibly unlikely event of these probes being picked up by another civilization, these greetings assure any aliens who manage to decode them that we are a peaceful planet and we wish any other beings in our Universe well.

There are different types of space probes and the type used for a particular mission will depend on the question that the probe is attempting to answer. Some probes fly by planets and take pictures for us, passing by several planets on their long journey. Others orbit a specific planet to gain more information about that planet and its moons. Another type of probe is designed to land and send back data from the surface of another world. Some of these are rovers, others remain fixed wherever they land.

The first rover, Lunokhod 1, was part of a Russian probe, Luna 17, which landed on the Moon in 1970. Lunokhod 1 was a robotic vehicle which could be steered from Earth, in much the same way as a remote control car.

NASA's Mars landers, Viking 1 and Viking 2, which touched down on the red planet in 1976, gave us our first pictures from the surface of the planet of War, which had intrigued people on Earth for millennia. The Viking landers showed the reddish-brown plains, scattered with rocks, the pink sky of Mars and even frost on the ground in winter. Unfortunately, it is very difficult to land on Mars and several probes sent to the red planet have crashed onto the surface.

ROBOTIC SPACE TRAVEL cont . . .

Later missions to Mars sent the two rovers, Spirit and Opportunity. Designed to drive around for at least three months, they lasted for far longer and also, like other spacecraft sent to Mars, found evidence that Mars had been shaped by the presence of water. In 2007, NASA sent the Phoenix Mission to Mars. Phoenix could not drive around Mars but it had a robotic arm to dig into the soil and collect samples. On board, it had a laboratory to examine the soil and work out what it contains. Mars also has three operational orbiters around it – the Mars Odyssey, Mars Express and Mars Reconnaissance Orbiter, showing us in detail the surface features.

Robotic space probes have also shown us the hellish world that lies beneath the thick atmosphere of Venus. Once it was thought that dense tropical forests might lie under the Venusian clouds but space probes have revealed the high temperatures, heavy carbon dioxide atmosphere and dark brown clouds of sulphuric acid. In 1990, NASA's Magellan entered orbit around Venus. Using radar to penetrate the atmosphere, Magellan mapped the surface of Venus and found 167 volcanoes larger than 70 miles wide! ESA's Venus Express has been in orbit around Venus since 2006. This mission is studying the atmosphere of Venus and trying to find out how Earth and Venus developed in such different ways. Several landers have returned information from the surface of Venus, a tremendous achievement given the challenges of landing on this most hostile of planets.

Robotic space probes have braved the scorched world of Mercury, a planet even closer to the Sun than Venus. Mariner 10, which flew by Mercury in 1974 and again in 1975, showed us that this bare little planet looks very similar to our Moon. It is a grey, dead planet with very little atmosphere. In 2008, the MESSENGER mission returned a space probe to Mercury and sent back the first new pictures of the Sun's nearest planet in 30 years.

Flying close to the Sun presents huge challenges for a robotic spacecraft but probes sent to the Sun – Helios 1, Helios 2, SOHO, TRACE, RHESSI and others – have sent back information which helped scientists to develop a far better understanding of the star at the very centre of our Solar System.

Further away in the Solar System, Jupiter was first seen in detail when the probe Pioneer 10 flew by in 1973. Pictures captured by Pioneer 10 also showed the Great Red Spot – a feature seen through telescopes

from Earth for centuries. After Pioneer, the Voyager probes revealed the surprising news about Jupiter's moons. Thanks to the Voyager probes, scientists on Earth learnt that Jupiter's moons are all very different to each other. In 1995, the Galileo probe arrived at Jupiter and spent eight years investigating the giant gas planet and its moons. Galileo was the first space probe to fly-by an asteroid, the first to discover an asteroid with a moon and the first to measure Jupiter over a long period of time. This amazing space probe also showed the volcanic activity on Jupiter's moon, Io, and found Europa to be covered in thick ice, beneath which may lie a gigantic ocean which could even harbour some form of life!

NASA's Cassini was not the first to visit Saturn – Pioneer 11 and the Voyager probes had flown past on their long journey and sent back detailed images of Saturn's rings and more information about the thick atmosphere on Titan. But when Cassini arrived in 2004 after a 7 year journey, it showed us many more features of Saturn and the moons that orbit it. Cassini also released a probe, ESA's Huygens, which travelled through the thick atmosphere to land on the surface of Titan. The Huygens probe discovered that Titan's surface is covered in ice and that methane rains down from the dense clouds.

Even further from Earth, Voyager 2 flew by Uranus and showed pictures of this frozen planet, tilted on its axis! Thanks to Voyager 2, we also know much more about the thin rings circling Uranus, which are very different to the rings of Saturn, as well as many other details of its moons. Voyager 2 carried on to Neptune and revealed this planet is very windy – Neptune has the fastest moving storms in the Solar System. Voyager 2 is now 10 billion miles from Earth and Voyager 1 is 11 billion miles away. They should be able to continue communicating with us until 2020.

The Stardust Mission – a probe which caught particles from a comet's tail and returned them to Earth in 2006 – taught us far more about the very early Solar System from these fragments. Capturing these samples from comets – which formed at the centre of the Solar System but have travelled to its very edge – has helped scientists to understand more about the origin of the Solar System itself.

'Where there is water,' Eric had told the kids, 'as we know from our planet Earth, there could be life!'

Even more importantly, Homer was to help prepare for a mission to Mars, which would take human beings to a new planet. For the first time ever, the Global Space Agency was getting ready to send a spacecraft with people on board to explore Mars and see if it would be possible to start a colony out there.

So Homer mattered a lot – not just because he was expensive or had fancy technology or, as Annie put it, looked like he had a personality, with his beady little camera eyes, stick legs and round tummy where the on-board oven lived.

Homer mattered because he was the first step into space for the human race – he was the front-runner for a whole new type of space exploration which might lead to people living on another planet.

On the day of Homer's descent to the red planet, they had stood in the big round control room, which was crammed with banks of computers and people eagerly reading the information from the screens. As he travelled, Homer sent back signals to Earth with progress reports. These arrived at the Global Space Agency in code, which the terrestrial computers then turned into words and pictures. Because of the time it took for Homer's signal to reach Earth, in the control room they were only discovering now what had happened on Mars. Had Homer landed – or had he crashed?

They were about to find out.

On the overhead screens, Annie and Emmett watched an animation of what was happening to Homer as he approached Mars. The atmosphere in the room was electric: groups of people stood nervously by, hoping that their robot had made it to the start of his mission.

It is very difficult to land on Mars, Eric explained. Mars has a thin atmosphere, which means it doesn't provide the natural braking that the Earth's atmosphere gives returning spacecraft. This meant Homer would be hurtling towards the surface of Mars at great speed and they would have to hope that all his systems worked properly to help him slow down; otherwise he would just crash down and end up as a pile of broken parts millions of miles away, with no one to fix him.

As Homer approached Mars's atmosphere, everyone was glued to the screens. To one side was a digital clock counting the time Homer had spent in space. Next to it, another time was displayed in UTC, the time system used by all space agencies to co-ordinate with each other and with their missions in space.

'We're watching the EDL now,' called out a serious-looking man wearing a headset.

'What's that?' asked Annie.

'Entry, descent and landing,' Emmett told her in a rather superior voice. 'Really, Annie, I thought you would have done some reading before we came, to get the most out of the experience.'

In reply, Annie trod firmly on Emmett's foot.

'Ouch! Ouch! Susan!' he cried. 'She's hurting me again!'

Susan gave her daughter a fierce look. Annie moved quietly away from Emmett to stand next to her dad. She slipped her hand into his. He was chewing his lip and frowning.

'Do you think Homer's landed?' she whispered.

'Hope so,' he said, smiling down at her. 'I mean, he's only a robot but he could send us some really useful information.'

'Atmospheric entry!' said the control operator.

When Homer – shaped a bit like an upside-down spinning top – broke through Mars's atmosphere, they saw the bright stream of flames erupting in his wake.

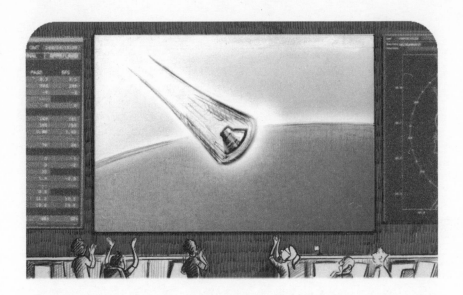

The room burst into applause.

'Peak heating rate in one minute and forty seconds,' warned the controller. 'Possible plasma blackout.' The room seemed to tense up automatically, as if everyone was holding their breath.

'Plasma blackout!' said the controller. 'We have plasma blackout! Expect signal to resume after two minutes.'

Annie squeezed her dad's hand.

He squeezed back. 'Don't worry,' he said. 'We know this happens sometimes – it's due to friction in the atmosphere.'

The clock on the wall ticked away as everyone in the room stared at it, waiting for contact to resume. Two minutes went by, then three, then four. People started to mutter to each other as the anxiety in the room mounted.

'We are receiving no signal from Homer,' said the controller. The screens showing Homer's descent had frozen as well. 'We have lost the signal to Homer!' said the controller. Red lights started flashing around the room.

'What's going on?' whispered Annie.

Her dad shook his head. 'I'm worried now,' he replied. 'There's a possibility that Homer's communication system melted during entry.'

'Does that mean Homer is dead?' asked Emmett loudly. Several people turned round to glare at him.

The controller had taken off his headset and was mopping his brow miserably. If Homer had no communication system, they had no way of knowing what had happened to their clever robot. He might have landed, he might have crashed. He might find evidence of life on Mars, but no one on Earth would ever know because he would never be able to send a signal and tell them.

'The Mars monitoring satellite shows no trace of Homer!' someone shouted, sounding like they were beginning to panic. 'The monitoring satellite cannot locate Homer. Homer has vanished from all systems.'

But then, just a few seconds later, Homer was back again. 'We have a signal!' exclaimed another man as his computer came to life. 'Homer approaching the surface of Mars. Homer deploying his parachute.'

On the TV screen they saw a parachute billowing out from behind Homer as the little robot swayed down to the planet's surface.

'Homer has landing legs prepared for touchdown. Homer has landed! Homer has reached the north polar region of Mars.'

Some people cheered – but Eric didn't. He looked puzzled.

'That's good, isn't it?' Annie whispered to him. 'Homer is OK.'

'Good, but weird,' said Eric, frowning. 'It doesn't make sense to me. Why did Homer lose the signal completely for so long and then bring it back? And why wasn't he showing up on the monitoring satellite? It's like he just disappeared for a few minutes. It's very strange. I wonder what is happening right now . . .'

Laika, the first living
Earth-born creature
in orbit.

Launch of the first US manned
space flight, May 1961.

Yuri Gagarin.

Launch of the Soviet spacecraft, Vostok I,
carrying Yuri Gagarin, April 1961.

Gemini rendezvous; Gemini VI spacecraft
photographed from Gemini VII, December 1965.

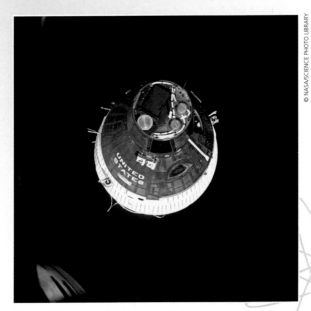

Gemini VII spacecraft photographed
from Gemini VI, December 1965.

EVA – astronaut emerging from command module.

Footprint of Neil Armstrong's first step on the Moon, July 20th 1969.

Apollo II astronaut Buzz Aldrin
walking on the moon.

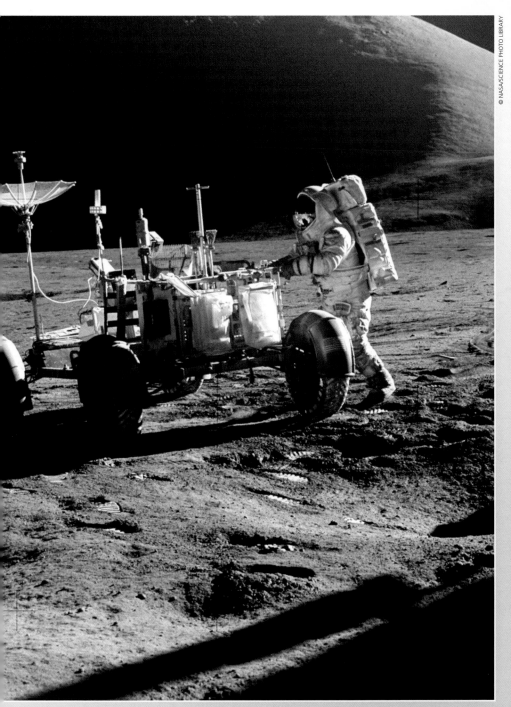

Astronaut James B. Irwin and lunar rover, Apollo 15, July 1971.

Above: Space shuttle simulator cockpit, 1999.

First Space Shuttle launch, 1981. The shuttle was called Columbia.

Astronaut floating in the International Space Station (ISS).

Below: ISS astronaut with fresh fruit in microgravity conditions.

© NASA/SCIENCE PHOTO LIBRARY

Astronauts making burgers aboard the ISS.

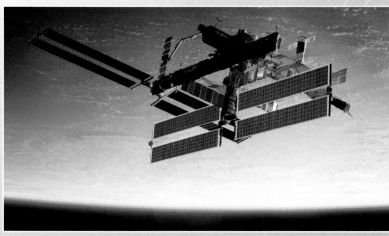

ISS with new solar panels, 2006.

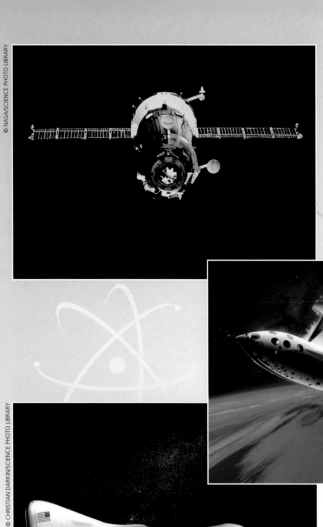

View of a Russian Soyuz spacecraft, photographed from a US space shuttle.

Above: SpaceShipOne re-entering the Earth's atmosphere from Orbit.

Computer artwork of SpaceShipOne, a private spacecraft, successfully launched into space in June 2004.

* * *

'So,' said George, who was now lying across the branch, 'what's this got to do with aliens?'

'Nothing,' said Emmett from below. 'She doesn't realize it was just a normal technical malfunction and she is making it into too big a deal.'

'That's because you don't know the rest of the story,' said Annie darkly. 'You don't know what happened next.'

'What?' said Emmett. 'What happened next?'

'It's not for crybabies and sneaks,' said Annie grandly. 'It's a story for big kids. So why don't you go inside and write some computer code while I talk to my friend.'

'Can you do that?' George asked Emmett. 'Can you really write computer code?'

'Oh yeah!' said Emmett enthusiastically. 'Anything you need on a computer, I can do it. I'm the code wizard. I applied for a job at a software firm a few months ago – I sent them some more information for an online version of my space shuttle simulator. They were going to give me a job. But then they found out I'm only nine years old. So they didn't.'

'So you're some kind of genius?' said George.

'Yup,' agreed Emmett happily. 'You can try my simulator, if you like. It shows you what it's like to go up in a spaceship. It's really cool. If you tell me the story about aliens, I'll let you both play.'

'We don't want to,' said Annie, just as George was thinking he'd love to have a go. 'So get lost!'

At the foot of the tree, Emmett burst into noisy sobs just as Susan and Eric came out onto the veranda.

'Tree time is over,' called Susan. 'And you three are coming in for dinner.'

Chapter 5

Georgewas so tired after his long journey that he
nearly fell asleep while cleaning his teeth. He
staggered into the room he was sharing with Emmett,
who was messing around on his computer, launching
spaceships on his simulator.

'Hey, George,' he said. 'Do you want to fly the
space shuttle? Look, it's really just like it is. I've put in all
the time commands too and it tells you what's
happening.'

'*T minus seven minutes and thirty seconds*,' said a
robotic voice from Emmett's computer. '*Orbiter access
arm retracted.*'

George was so exhausted he could hardly speak. 'No,
Emmett,' he said, 'I think I'll just . . .' And he fell asleep
to the countdown of a spaceship launch.

The commands from the space-shuttle launch must
have wormed their way into George's brain because
he had a strange dream. He dreamed he was in the
Commander's seat on the shuttle, responsible for

flying the huge great spacecraft into space. It felt like being strapped to the top of an enormous rocket and sent up into the heavens. As they flew into the darkness of space, he thought he saw stars flashing at him through the shuttle window. In the darkness outside, they suddenly looked very bright and very close. One of them seemed to be zooming towards him, shining a bright light directly into his face, so close and so brilliant that—

He woke up with a start and found himself in an unfamiliar bed with someone flashing a torch in his face.

'George!' the figure hissed. 'George! Get up! It's an emergency!'

It was Annie in her pyjamas.

'Bleeeuurgh!' exclaimed George, shielding his eyes from the light as she threw back his duvet and grabbed him by the arm.

'Downstairs,' she said. 'And super-quietly. It's our only chance to escape Emmett! Come on!'

George blundered after her, his mind still reeling from his strange dream about flying the space shuttle. He tiptoed down the stairs to the kitchen, where Annie opened the door and led him out onto the veranda. She shone her torch on a piece of paper.

The piece of paper had drawings all over it. It looked like this:

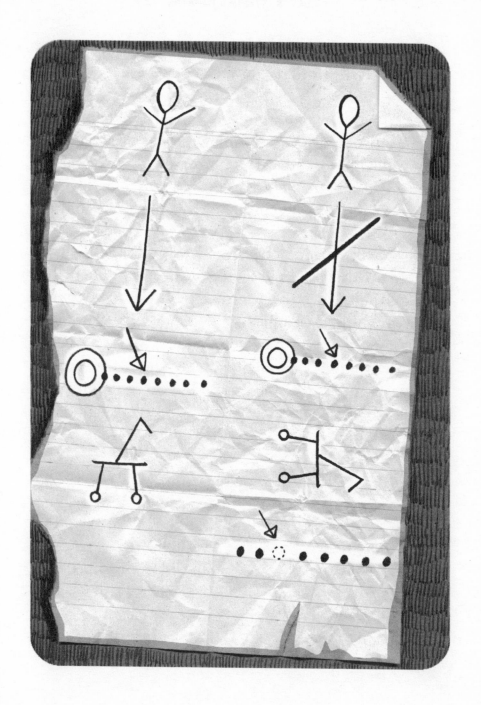

'This is it?' said George, blinking. 'This is the alien message? They sent it to you on a piece of school note-book paper?'

'No, twit,' Annie told him. 'Of course they didn't. I got this through Cosmos! I copied it from his screen.'

'Cosmos?' George exclaimed. 'But he doesn't work.'

'I know!' said Annie. 'But I didn't finish the story.'

After Homer had landed on Mars, the robot was supposed to start doing all sorts of clever things, like taking readings of the Martian weather, looking for water in the soil samples and other signs that there might be some form of bacterial life on Mars.

But he wouldn't do any of them. The robot seemed to have gone crazy. He refused to respond to any signals from Earth; he just drove round in circles or threw scoopfuls of mud into the air.

Even though he wasn't replying to their signals, Homer carried on sending messages, which turned out to be pictures of his tyres and other useless bits of information. From Earth, they could see the robot – but only sometimes – via the monitoring satellite that orbited Mars and sent back pictures. Once, Annie said, her dad had been watching Homer and he'd picked up something really odd on the satellite pictures. He said that if he hadn't known better, he would have sworn that Homer was waving his robotic arm at him. It was almost like Homer was trying to attract his attention.

Eric, Annie said, was getting really stressed out by all this. Lots of people wanted to know what Homer had found on Mars and what he was doing up there. But so far they had nothing to show except a robot behaving in a very silly fashion.

It was putting the Global Space Agency in an awkward position. Homer was an extremely expensive robot and it took many people to build, launch and operate him. He was an important part of the new space programme as he was meant to blaze the trail for human beings to go out and live on a different planet. So the fact that he didn't seem to work properly meant that those who weren't in favour of the space programme or sending astronauts far out into space could argue that this was all a big waste of time.

Homer's bad behaviour also meant that Eric wasn't getting the information he was hoping for about possible life on Mars. It was breaking his heart to see his robot mess around on the red planet. Day by day he looked sadder and sadder. If Homer didn't start co-operating soon, the mission would be abandoned and the robot would become just a pile of metal on a distant planet.

Annie couldn't bear it. Her dad had been so excited and happy at the prospect of receiving Homer's findings. She hated seeing him so upset. So she had a brilliant idea: she decided to get Cosmos out of retirement, just to see if she could make him work again.

'I realized that if we had Cosmos,' she told George as they stood outside under the starry sky, 'we could just nip off to Mars, sort out the robot and come home again without anyone even knowing. If we went when the monitoring satellite was on the other side of Mars, no one would even see us. I mean, we'd have to be careful not to leave a footprint or drop anything. That would be a bit of a disaster.'

'Hmm,' said George, still affected by his weird dream. 'So what did you do?'

'I got Cosmos out of his secret hiding place.'

'Not that secret if you knew about it,' said George.

'And,' Annie went on, ignoring him, 'I started him up.'

'And he actually worked?' George was wide awake now.

'Not really,' admitted Annie. 'At least, only for a few seconds, and he didn't say anything. But this is what I saw on his screen.' She waved the paper at George. 'It was there – honest, it was. It was a message – I checked Sender ID and it said: *Unknown*. For message location, it said: *Extra-terrestrial*. Then Cosmos died and I couldn't start him up again.'

'Wow!' said George. 'Did you tell Eric?'

'Of course,' said Annie. 'And he tried to start Cosmos

up again but couldn't. I showed him the message but he didn't believe me.' She pouted. 'He said I was making up stories – but I'm sure Homer really is waving to us and has something he wants to tell us. But my dad just insisted that Homer doesn't work because he had a bad atmospheric entry and that this message – if Cosmos received it at all – is just something to do with Cosmos being broken.'

'But that's really boring of him!' remarked George.

'No, he's just being a scientist. It's like Emmett said,' admitted Annie: 'most people believe there is only some form of bacteria out there and no real aliens.

But I think . . .'

'What do you think?' asked George, looking up at the stars.

'I think,' said Annie firmly, 'that someone out there is trying to get in touch with us. I think someone is using Homer to attract our attention, and because we're just ignoring him, they've started sending us messages instead. Only we can't pick them up because Cosmos isn't working.'

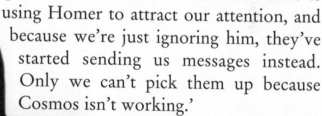

'What are we going to do?'

'We've got to go out there,' said Annie, 'and see for ourselves. But first we have to mend Cosmos. We need to see if the aliens are sending us any more messages! And then, maybe, we can send one back . . .'

'How would we do that?' asked George. 'I mean, how can we send a message that they will understand? And even if we knew how to send it, what would we say? And in what language? They've sent us the message in pictures – it must be because they don't know how to speak to us.'

'I think we're going to say, *Leave our lovely robot alone, you pesky aliens!*' said Annie, looking fierce. *'You're messing with the wrong civilization! Pick on someone else!'*

'But we want to know who they are and where they come from,' protested George. 'We can't just say *Get lost, aliens* and never find out who sent the message.'

'What about, *Come in peace and then go home?*' said Annie. 'So we find out who they are but they're not allowed to come to Earth if they have evil intentions.'

'Yeah?' said George. 'Who's going to stop them? They could land here and be like huge scary machines who stamp us into the ground, just like we do with ants.'

'Or,' said Annie, her eyes shining in the torchlight, 'they might be teeny-weeny, like little wriggly bacteria under a microscope. Only they don't realize how large we are and so we don't even notice when they arrive.'

'They might have fourteen heads and dribble slime,' said George ghoulishly. 'We'd notice that!'

They heard a creaking noise, followed by footsteps on the stairs. A bleary-eyed Eric came out onto the veranda.

'What's going on here?' he said rather crossly.

'George couldn't sleep,' said Annie quickly. 'Because of the jet lag. So I was just, um, getting him a glass of water.'

'Hmm,' said Eric, his hair sticking up all over the place. 'Upstairs with you both now.'

George sneaked into the room he shared with Emmett and hopped back into bed, but not before he'd pinched Annie's torch from her. He was wide awake now so he got out his copy of *The User's Guide* and turned to the chapter: 'How to Talk to Aliens'.

GETTING IN TOUCH WITH ALIENS

If aliens are really out there, will we ever get to meet them?

The distances between the stars are staggeringly great, so we still can't be sure that a face-to-face encounter will someday take place (assuming the aliens have faces!). But even if extraterrestrials never visit our planet or receive a visit from us, we might still get to know one another. We might still be able to talk.

One way this could happen is by radio. Unlike sound, radio waves can move through the empty spaces between the stars. And they move as fast as anything *can* move – at the speed of light.

Almost 50 years ago, some scientists worked out what it would take to send a signal from one star system to another. It surprised them to learn that interstellar conversation wouldn't require super-advanced technology like you often see in science-fiction films. It's possible to send radio signals from one solar system to another with the type of radio equipment we could build today. So the scientists stood back from their chalkboards and said to themselves: If this is so easy, then no matter what aliens might be doing, they'd surely be using radio to communicate over large distances. The scientists realized that it would be a perfectly logical idea to turn some of our big antennae to the skies and see if we could pick up extraterrestrial signals. After all, finding an alien broadcast would instantly prove that there's someone out there, without the expense of sending rockets to distant star systems in the hope of discovering a populated planet.

Unfortunately, this alien eavesdropping experiment, called SETI (the Search for Extraterrestrial Intelligence), has so far failed to find a single, sure peep from the skies. The radio bands have been discouragingly quiet wherever we've looked, aside from the natural static caused by such objects as quasars (the churning, high-energy centres of some galaxies) or pulsars (rapidly spinning neutron stars).

Does that mean that intelligent aliens, able to build radio transmitters, don't exist? That would be an astounding discovery, because there are surely at least a million million planets in our Milky Way Galaxy – and there are 100 thousand million *other* galaxies! If no one is out there, we are stupendously special, and dreadfully alone.

Well, as SETI researchers will tell you, it's entirely too soon to conclude that we have no company among the stars. After all, if you're going to listen for alien radio broadcasts, not only do you have to point your antenna in the right direction, but you also need to tune to the right spot on the dial, have a sensitive enough receiver, and be listening at the right time. SETI experiments are like looking for buried treasure without a map. So the fact that we haven't found anything so far isn't surprising. It's like digging a few holes on the beach of a South Pacific island and coming up with nothing but wet sand and crabs. You shouldn't immediately conclude that there's no treasure to be found.

Fortunately, new radio telescopes are speeding up our search for signals, and it's possible that within a few dozen years we could hear a faint broadcast from another civilization.

What would they be saying to us? Well, of course we can only guess, but one thing the extra-terrestrials will surely know: they'd better send us a long message, because speedy conversation is simply impossible. For example, imagine that the nearest aliens are on a planet around a star that's 1,000 light years away. If we pick up a signal from them tomorrow, it will have taken 1,000 years to get to us.

It will be an old message, but that's OK. After all, if you read Sophocles or Shakespeare, those are old 'messages' too, but they're still interesting.

However, if we choose to reply, our response to the aliens will take 1,000 years to get to them, and another 1,000 years will pass before their answer gets back to us! In other words, even a simple 'Hello?' and its alien response, 'Zork?' would take 20 centuries. So while talking on the radio is a lot faster than travelling in rockets for a meet-and-greet, it's still going to be a very relaxed conversation. That suggests that the aliens might send us books and books of stuff about themselves and their planet, knowing that we won't be doing a lot of chatting.

But even if they do, even if they send us *The Alien Encyclopaedia*, will we be able to read it? After all, unlike in the movies and TV, the extraterrestrials aren't going to be fluent in English or any other earthly language. It's possible that they may use pictures or even mathematics to help make their message understandable, but we won't know until and unless we pick up a signal.

No matter what they send us, detecting a radio squeal coming from a distant world would be big news. Indeed, imagine what it was like five centuries ago when explorers first discovered that there were entire continents, filled with inhabitants, that were completely unknown in Europe. Finding the New World changed everything.

Today, we've replaced the wooden sailing ships of those early explorers with giant aluminium-and-steel antennae. Someday soon they may tell us something extraordinarily interesting: namely, that in the vast expanses of space, humans are not the only ones watching the Universe.

And today's young people may be those who will be there to listen – and to respond. This could mean *you*!

Seth

Chapter 6

The next morning at breakfast, George's eyelids were very heavy and he felt rather confused to be eating breakfast at the time he'd usually be having lunch. However, that felt like nothing compared to Annie's revelations from the night before. He didn't know what to make of what she'd told him.

Once before, George hadn't believed her: when he first met Annie and she had told him she went on journeys around the Solar System, he had laughed at her and said she was lying. But that had turned out to be true in the end, so he wondered what to make of this latest story.

It worried him that, according to Annie, Eric didn't seem to be taking the alien message seriously. On the other hand, if it meant he might get a trip out to space, just to check it out, he felt he would probably go along with Annie's version. Anything to fly through the cosmos again, even if it was on a fruitless quest for an alien life form!

Susan suddenly spoke up. 'I thought we'd show

George the neighbourhood today,' she said. 'Take him around and maybe go to the beach.'

Annie looked stricken. 'Mum!' she said. 'George and I have stuff to do here.'

'And I've got my theories on the information-loss paradox to work on,' said Emmett rather sourly. 'Not that anyone cares.'

'Don't be daft,' said Susan firmly. 'George has come a long way to see us and we can't expect him to just sit in a tree, chatting to you all day.' The phone rang and she answered it. 'George, it's for you,' she said, passing over the receiver.

'George!' came the crackly voice of his dad, sounding like he was shouting from a very long way away. 'Just wanted to let you know we've arrived in Tuvalu! We're just about to get on the ship and sail for the atolls. How's it going in Florida?'

'It's fine!' said George. 'I'm here with Eric and Susan and Annie and this other boy called Emmett who is—'

But the connection cut off. George handed the phone back to Susan.

'I'm sure he'll call again,' she reassured him. 'And your mum and dad know you are OK. Now we're going to go out and have lots of fun!'

Annie rolled her eyes at George, but there was no getting out of it. Her mum had made plans to take them to the funfair, to the pool, to a dolphin sanctuary, to the beach. They were out all day and all evening for several days. There was no opportunity for them to get Cosmos out of his secret hiding place and work on him. And with Emmett constantly trailing their every move, they hardly even had a chance to look at Annie's alien message – only the once, when they locked themselves into the bathroom and studied the piece of paper.

'So, that's a person,' said Annie. 'And that arrow must mean the person is going somewhere. But where?'

'Um, the person is going to . . .' said George. 'A series of small dots moving around a bigger dot. I know! What if the dots are the planets in orbit around the Sun, which is at the centre? The arrow points to the fourth dot, so it means the person is going to the fourth planet from the Sun, which is—'

'Mars!' said Annie. 'I *knew* it! There *is* a link to Homer. This message means we have to go to Mars and—'

'But what does the rest mean?' said George. 'What does all this mean – a person with an arrow crossed out?'

'Perhaps that's what will happen if the person *doesn't* go to Mars?'

'If the person doesn't go to Mars,' said George, looking down the column, 'then the funny-looking stick insect falls over.'

'Funny-looking stick insect . . .' said Annie. 'What if that's Homer? If the person doesn't go to Mars, maybe something terrible will happen to Homer. We have to get out there and save Homer! It's really important!'

'Look, Annie,' said George doubtfully, 'I know your dad's upset about Homer but he is just a robot. They could send another one. I just don't know that these messages are enough to prove anything.'

'Look at the last line,' said Annie in a spooky voice. 'And be afraid.'

'If the person doesn't go to Mars and doesn't save Homer, then . . .' said George.

'No planet Earth,' said Annie.

'No planet Earth?' exclaimed George.

'No planet Earth,' confirmed Annie. 'That's what the message means. We have to go to Mars to save Homer because if we don't, something terrible will happen to this planet.'

'We have to tell your dad,' said George urgently. 'I've tried,' said Annie. 'You have a go.'

At that moment they heard a banging on the bathroom door.

'Come out!' shouted Emmett. 'Resistance is futile!'

'Can I flush his head down the toilet?' said Annie longingly.

'No!' said George sharply. 'You can't. He's not a bad kid – he's really nice if you bother actually to talk to him . . .'

Emmett started bashing on the door again.

At last Annie's mum decided they all needed a quiet day at home. The next day was to be the great highlight of George's visit. Eric had got them tickets to see the launch of the space shuttle! They were going to the launch pad to watch the mighty spacecraft blast off from Earth. Even Emmett got thoroughly over-excited. He kept muttering space-shuttle commands to himself and reciting facts about orbital velocity.

George and Annie were both thrilled for different reasons. George was gripped by the idea of the enormous rocket that gave the space shuttle the power it needed to zoom upwards into space. In the past, he had walked through Cosmos's doorway to travel through space; now he was going to watch a real spacecraft begin its great journey!

As for Annie, she was fizzing with secretive joy over the idea of the launch. 'My plan is coming together,' she whispered to George. 'We will uncover the aliens!

We will!' Annoyingly, she refused to explain to George quite how she meant to do this. When he asked her, she got a faraway look in her eyes. 'It's all in the plan,' she told him. 'And when you need to know, then I will tell you. For now, you must believe.' It was very irritating for George and he much preferred talking to Emmett than to Annie when she was in full-on mystery mode.

Even so, the more she stalked about impersonating a secret agent working on extraterrestrial activity, the more George racked his brains as to what the alien message might mean and where it had come from. He had tried talking to Eric about it but he hadn't got far.

'George,' Eric said patiently, 'I'm sorry that I don't believe that an evil alien life form is messing around with my robot or wanting to destroy the Earth, but I don't. So please leave it. I've got other things on my mind. Like how to send another robot out to Mars to take over the work that Homer should have done. This has been a terrible time for us at the Global Space Agency. Not everyone is as keen on space travel as you and Annie. Some people don't accept that it has any use at all.'

'But what about all the inventions that have come from space?' said George hotly. 'If we hadn't gone into space, there's so much stuff we wouldn't have now on Earth.'

SPACE INVENTIONS

There are many things we use on Earth that have been improved or developed because of advances in space technology. Here are just some of them:

- air purification
- anti-fog ski goggles
- automatic insulin pumps
- bone-analyser technology
- car brake linings, better ones
- cataract-surgery tools
- composite golf clubs
- corrosion protection coating
- Dustbuster
- earthquake prediction system
- energy-saving air conditioning
- fire resistant materials
- fire/flame detectors
- flat-panel televisions
- food packaging
- freeze-dried technology
- high-density batteries
- home security systems
- improvements in imaging using MRI
- lead poison detection
- miniaturized circuits
- noise abatement
- pollution measuring devices
- portable x-ray devices
- programmable pacemakers
- protective clothing
- radioactive-leak detectors
- robotic hands
- satellite navigation
- school bus design (improved)
- scratch-resistant lenses
- sewage treatment
- shock-absorbing helmets
- smokestack monitors
- solar energy systems
- storm warning services (Doppler radar)
- studless winter tyres
- swimming-pool purification systems
- toothpaste tubes

'And,' continued Eric gently, 'even if we could get Cosmos working, after all that computer has been through, I don't think it's safe to use the portal. What if he broke down when someone was out there in space and we couldn't get him started again in time to rescue them? Homer is only a robot, George. It isn't worth the risk.'

'But what about the end of the message?' persisted George. 'With the Earth crossed out?'

'It probably comes from some crank,' said Eric. 'And there are plenty of them. Don't think about it any more. I will get Homer sorted out – somehow. And the planet isn't coming to an end, not for several billions of years, when our Sun comes to the end of its life. So there's no panic.'

'Finally!' said Annie when her dad went to work, her mum popped out for a few minutes and Emmett seemed safely absorbed with his online simulator. 'We can work on Operation Alien Life Form. We don't have long. And we *have* to get Cosmos working before tomorrow. It's crucial. Come on, George!' She ran up the stairs to her parents' room.

George followed her, grumbling as he went. 'Are you actually going to tell me what we're doing?' he demanded from outside her parents' bedroom. 'I'm sick of you saying, "It's on a need-to-know basis and you don't need to know." I came over because you said you needed my help. So far you've hardly told me anything about your plan.'

Annie emerged beaming from her parents' room, holding a metal box. 'I'm sorry!' she whispered. 'But I didn't want you to tell Emmett about us going into space to chase aliens.'

'I wouldn't!' said George, feeling hurt that she didn't trust him.

Annie barged her way into her bedroom and put the metal box down on her desk. 'Cosmos,' she announced, 'is in here. And I have the key.' She produced a tiny little key on a chain around her neck, then opened the box and pulled out the familiar flat silver computer. She locked the box again and took it back to the wardrobe in her parents' room.

'How did you get the key?' asked George when she returned.

'I borrowed it,' said Annie mysteriously. 'After I got Cosmos out and received the alien message, Dad decided to lock him away. But he doesn't realize how clever I am.'

'Or how sneaky?' commented George.

'Whatever,' said Annie. 'Let's get on.'

She opened up Cosmos and plugged him in. She pressed ENTER – the secret key to the Universe – but nothing happened. She pressed it again but the screen stayed blank.

Suddenly her bedroom door inched open and a nose poked round it.

'What are you doing?' said Emmett.

'Nothing!' said Annie, jumping up to try and block his view. But Emmett had already edged his way in.

'If you don't tell me what you're doing with that computer,' he said slyly, 'I'll tell your mum and dad.'

'Tell them what?' said Annie.

'I'll tell them whatever it is you're doing that you don't want me – or them – to know about.'

'But you don't know what I'm doing,' said Annie.

'Yes, I do,' said Emmett. 'That computer is the one you think is really powerful. The one you're not meant to use by yourselves. I've been listening to you and George when you don't think I can hear you.'

'You little worm!' screamed Annie, throwing herself at Emmett.

'I hate you!' he yelled back, tussling with her.

'I never wanted to come here for the holidays! I wanted to go to Silicon Valley with my mum and dad. This is the worst summer of my life!'

'JUST SHUT UP, BOTH OF YOU!' shouted George.

Annie and Emmett let go of each other and gazed at the normally mild-mannered George in surprise.

'Now look here,' he said. 'You're both being ridiculous. Emmett's having a horrible holiday and he's really bored. But you're a computer genius, right, Emmett?'

'Affirmative,' said Emmett sulkily.

'And, Annie – you've got a computer problem you can't solve. So why don't you ask Emmett – nicely – if he'll take a look at Cosmos and see if he knows what to do with him? He might enjoy doing it and we might be able to stop fighting. OK?'

'S'pose so,' grumbled Annie.

'Right,' said George. 'Annie – you explain.'

She pointed to the silver laptop lying on her bed. 'This is a computer—'

'I can see that.' Emmett scowled.

She ploughed on: '– that can do special things. Like open doorways to places in space.'

Emmett looked down his nose. 'I doubt that.'

'No, it can,' said George. 'The computer has a name – he's called Cosmos and when he works, he's amazing. Eric invented him but we blew him up by mistake last year. Now, Eric really needs Cosmos and we need you to get him working again. Emmett, do you think you could try and mend him?'

'I'll get my emergency computer kit!' said Emmett, who was now beaming from ear to ear. He dashed out of the door.

'He's not so bad,' said George to Annie. 'Just give him a chance.'

'Just the *one*,' muttered Annie.

Emmett came back with a collection of hardware, CDs and screwdrivers of different sizes. He arranged them all in neat piles and started fiddling around with Cosmos. The others watched him in silence, noticing how the smug look on his face faded as he grappled with their old friend. A frown crept over his brow.

'Wow!' he remarked. 'I have never seen anything like this! I didn't think they could make a computer I didn't understand!'

'Can you save him?' whispered Annie.

Emmett looked baffled. 'This hardware is mega-cool,' he said. 'And I thought quantum computing was just a theory.' He twiddled a bit more, biting his lip in concentration.

The noise of cicadas buzzing in the garden floated in from the window. But suddenly they heard another sound. It was very faint and none of them could be absolutely sure they'd really heard it.

'Wasn't that—?'

'Shush!' said Annie. They heard it again. A very quiet *beep*. When they looked closely at the great computer, they realized that a tiny yellow light on one side of him had come on. In the middle of his screen, which until now had been blank, they saw a thin line appear.

'Emmett!' squeaked Annie, hugging him enthusiastically – he flinched away and pulled a face. 'You did it! I'm going to try talking to him.' She leaned towards the screen. 'Cosmos, please come back!' she pleaded. 'We *need* you.'

The screen flickered and then went dull. But then Cosmos beeped again – once, and then twice. And another line appeared across the centre of his screen. The line turned into a squiggle for a few seconds, and then a circle, and then disappeared.

'This is weird,' said Emmett slowly. He punched in a few commands. He pressed a few more keys and sat back.

There was a whirring noise. And then, finally, Cosmos spoke.

'1010111110000010,' he said.

George and Annie were stunned into silence. It had never occurred to them that they might get Cosmos working but then not understand what he said.

'11000101001,' Cosmos continued.

Annie tugged Emmett's shirt.

'What have you done to him?' she asked him, her face a picture of panic. 'Where's the alien message?'

'Holy supersymmetric strings!' exclaimed Emmett. 'He's speaking Base Two!'

'What's that?' said George.

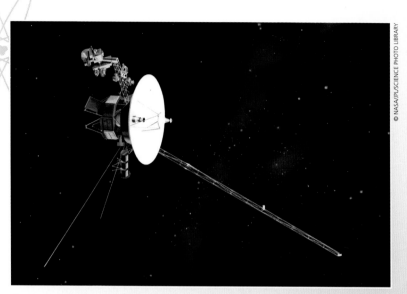

© NASA/JPL/SCIENCE PHOTO LIBRARY

Computer artwork of the Voyager spacecraft.

© J NASA/JPL/UA/LOCKHEED MARTIN/SCIENCE PHOTO LIBRARY

Computer artwork of the Phoenix spacecraft on Mars.

Image of the Chasma Boreale canyon on Mars.

Mercury

The cratered surface of the planet Mercury.

Below: Craters on Mercury.

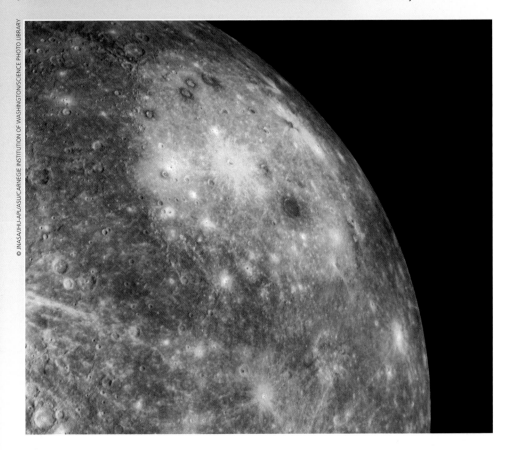

Venus

Volcanoes on Venus.

© JPL/NASA/SCIENCE PHOTO LIBRARY

Venus' atmosphere.

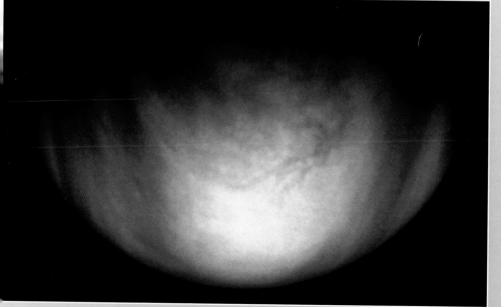

Jupiter

Voyager 1 image of Jupiter.

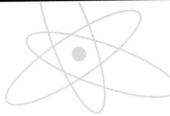

Saturn

© NASA/SCIENCE PHOTO LIBRARY

Voyager 1 image of Saturn and its
ring system.

© NASA/JPL/SSI/SCIENCE PHOTO LIBRARY

Cassini image of Saturn's moon,
Titan, in front of Saturn.

Uranus and Neptune

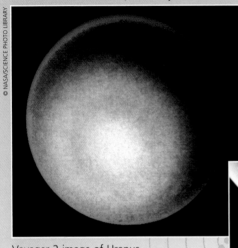

Voyager 2 image of Uranus.

Below: Voyager 2 image of Neptune with its largest moon, Triton, just visible.

Voyager 2 image of Neptune.

'It's a positional notation with a radix of two,' said Emmett. 'It's binary – the system used internally by all computers.'

George tried typing a command on the screen but jumped back as Cosmos screeched, '1010001010111 0101010001010101010110101000001 0010101.'

'What?' said Annie. 'What's happening to Cosmos? Why can he speak but we don't know what he's saying?'

'So this 'puter, like, it speaks to you and you understand it . . . ?' said Emmett slowly. 'Cos now he's speaking the underlying system, the one underneath a computer language. Like a pre-language.'

'1101011!' wailed Cosmos.

'Oh my gosh!' gasped Annie. 'What if it's like he's become a little baby computer, and he's speaking baby language?'

Cosmos gurgled. And then laughed.

'So he could just be saying "'Poon! Dada! Mama",' Annie continued.

'I think you're right,' said Emmett, who was too busy staring at the screen to notice he'd just agreed with Annie. 'I'll try him on something. Let's see if he knows Basic.'

'GOTO GOTO GOTO GOTO,' said Cosmos.

Emmett inserted a disk into the super-computer. 'I'll try to update him on something harder,' he said. 'Something more up-to-date. It's like he's in an ancient computer world right now. I'll try FORTRAN 95.'

0
1
0
0
1
1
0
1
0
1
0
1
0
1
0
1
0
1
0

1
0
0
1
1
0
1
0
1
0
1
0
1
0
1

Our normal numerical system works with a base of 10. There are numbers from 1 to 9 and then the number 1 moves into the next 'column' to show that there is one group of 'ten's. After 99 (9 x 10 plus 9 x 1), a new column is needed to show the amount of 100s (10 x 10); then again for 1000s (10 x 10 x 10) after 999 is reached. And so on.

With binary, the base is 2 instead of 10, so that the columns will represent multiples of 2 ie: 2, 4 (2 x 2), 8 (2 x 2 x 2) etc. The number three therefore appears as 11 (1 x 2 plus 1 x 1). And counting 1 to 10 becomes 1, 10, 11, 100, 101, 110, 111, 1000, 1001, 1010.

Early computer programmers decided to use binary code because it is simpler to design a circuit with either 'on' or 'off' positions than one with many alternative states. Binary code works on the principle that the early computers were constructed using electrical systems that recognized on or off positions only – which could be represented by using O for 'off' and 1 for 'on'. In this way complicated calculations could be translated into on/off circuits throughout the computer.

0 0100110001110101010110 1

'REAL. NOT. END. DO,' replied the super-computer.

Emmett tried once more and Cosmos's screen dimmed and his circuits fizzed. 'He is gobbling up these disks,' said Emmett. 'Spooky, huh?'

Finally Cosmos spoke in a language they could understand. ''S up?' he asked.

'Cosmos!' said Annie excitedly. 'You're back. That's great news! Now, I need you to open up the portal, quick as you can. I need to have a look—'

'Nim nim nim,' said Cosmos lazily.

George jumped in. 'Cosmos!' he pleaded. 'We're in deep trouble. We really need you to help us.'

'Yeah, I'm just jammin', innit,' replied the world's most intelligent computer.

'You're doing what?' said George slowly, bending down to take a closer look at him.

'Eh, don't look at my screen!' shouted Cosmos suddenly. 'Don't look, man, dat stuff's private.'

George tried again. 'We've got a big problem—' he began.

'Shut up,' Cosmos interrupted him. 'I'm busy. And don't be lookin' at ma screen or nothin'.'

'Cosmos . . .' cooed Annie gently. 'Why are you so vexed?'

'Cos I don't want to roll with these dry people,' he replied. 'But you're on a level.'

'Praise!' said Annie. 'But, Cosmos, you ledge, it's like kronik here right now. My dad's, like, flat roofin' cos someone's, like, jooked his robot.'

'That's so raw!' exclaimed Cosmos, finally sounding interested.

George and Emmett listened in complete bewilderment as Annie chatted to the computer.

'You're the uber beast computer!' said Annie. 'Can you help us find out who scaved our robot?'

'Yeah, all right,' replied Cosmos. 'I'm on it.'

As he whirred away, Annie turned to face the others with a rather smug grin on her face.

'He said I was on a level!' she exclaimed happily. 'And look . . .' she breathed. 'The door to the Universe!'

A little beam of light had shot out from Cosmos's screen, and on the other side of the room he was drawing the doorway through which George and Annie had once walked into the Universe. The door swung open, and behind it they saw a dark sky peppered with stars that shone much more brightly than when they were seen from Earth.

A red planet was coming into view.

George took a step towards the portal, but before he could get any closer, the door slammed shut in his face. On it was pinned a large poster with the words KEEP OUT in big wonky letters. They all jumped as loud electronic music started blaring from behind the door.

'Annie, what's going on?' asked George.

'Well, I'm not really sure,' she said. 'But Cosmos sounds like the older kids at my school back home – I mean, he's speaking the way they do when they think they're really cool.'

'How old are these kids?' asked George.

'Oh, about fourteen, I suppose,' said Annie. 'Why?'

'Because,' said George, who had worked it out, 'Cosmos started out with baby computer language when we first got him going. And Emmett moved him on but couldn't update him totally. So that means that now—'

Annie finished the sentence for him:

'Cosmos,' she said in fear and wonder, 'is a *teenager*.'

'What's your dad going to say?' asked George.

'I think we'd better not tell him. At least, not yet.'

They heard the front door open downstairs. 'Quick!' said Annie. 'Emmett, close Cosmos down!'

Emmett shut down the computer and they shoved Cosmos under Annie's bed. Footsteps came up the stairs and when Eric opened the door to Annie's bedroom, he found the three kids sitting in a row, looking at a book he had written.

'Nice to see you all getting along,' he remarked.

Annie slung an arm round Emmett's shoulders. 'Oh yes,' she said. 'We're friends now, aren't we?' She poked him lightly. 'Speak,' she whispered in his ear.

'Yes, I can confirm that,' said Emmett mechanically. He hadn't yet recovered from seeing Cosmos open up the portal.

'Good, good,' said Eric. 'I see you're reading one of my books. *The Large-scale Structure of Spacetime.* How are you finding it?'

'It's very interesting,' said George politely. He hadn't understood a word of it.

Emmett came back to life. 'You've made an error on page one hundred and thirty-six,' he said helpfully.

'Is that so?' said Eric, smiling. 'No one's ever spotted that before but that doesn't mean you're wrong.'

'I have a suggestion as to how to rectify it,' said Emmett.

Annie groaned, but George gave her a stern look. 'I mean, well done, Emmett,' she said.

'OK, good,' said Eric slowly. 'I was going to suggest we all go out for an ice cream. But if you're all absorbed, then I won't disturb you any further—'

'Ice cream!' Annie and George jumped up. Emmett stayed sitting on the bed, his eyes still glued to the book.

'Earth to Emmett!' said Annie. 'Ice cream! You know, the cold sweet stuff that kids like! Let's go have one!'

Emmett looked up, unsure. 'Do you actually want me to come too?' he said.

'Yes!' said Annie and George. 'We do!'

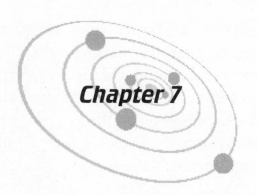

Chapter 7

The next day dawned beautiful and calm, the perfect day to set off into space. Annie woke George and Emmett up early.

'It's space-shuttle day!' she shrieked into George's ear. He groaned and turned over under his duvet. 'Get up, get up!' she said, pulling the duvet off him and dancing around the room with it. 'This is the most exciting day of our lives!'

Emmett had sat bolt upright in bed. 'I'm so happy I might be—' He jumped out of bed and ran into the bathroom.

Annie grabbed one of George's hands and pulled him to his feet as he blearily tried to wake up. Emmett tottered back in, looking rather pale.

'Tree!' Annie said to both of them. 'Now! We've got planning to do.'

Still in their pyjamas, they scrambled downstairs and out onto the veranda. George shinned up the tree and Annie swiftly followed him, leaving Emmett standing forlornly at the foot.

'Come on, Emmett,' said Annie. 'Get up here!'

'I can't,' said Emmett miserably.

'Why not?'

'I've never climbed a tree,' he admitted. 'I don't know how.'

'Oh, for heaven's sakes!' exclaimed Annie. 'What have you been doing with yourself?'

'Writing computer programs,' said Emmett sadly. 'By myself.'

Annie sighed noisily but George dropped out of the tree in one single fluid movement, grabbed Emmett and hoisted him up. He pushed from below and Annie pulled from above, and with some squeaking and scraping they propelled the smaller boy onto the big branch. Emmett looked down nervously.

'Now then,' Annie told him sternly, 'we are going to have an

adventure today. We are going to be brave and amazing. And hopefully we are going to save planet Earth. And that means no crying or whingeing or running to my mum. Do you understand, Emmett?'

Emmett nodded while clinging tightly to the branch. 'Yes, Annie,' he said meekly.

'You're our friend now,' Annie told him. 'So if you have something to say, you tell me or George – you don't go charging off to a grown-up.'

'Yes, Annie,' he agreed, giving her a little smile. 'I've never had a friend before.'

'Well, now you've got two,' said George.

'And we're going to need you,' added Annie. 'You are super-important to the masterplan, Emmett. Don't let us down.'

He gasped. 'I won't!' he said. 'I absolutely totally and utterly will not!'

'OK, great!' said George. 'That's all great! But what in fact, Annie, *are* we going to do?'

'We are going,' she said, 'on a great cosmic journey. So listen up, savers of planet Earth, and prepare to meet the Universe. I'm going to tell you the masterplan: we're going to change out of our pyjamas, pack up Cosmos, find my dad and get to the Global Space Agency. And that's where it will all begin.'

The first step of their cosmic journey, Annie explained, took them to the launch pad at the Global Space Agency, where they would be watching the space shuttle launch.

MANNED SPACE FLIGHT

'The Eagle has landed!

This is the message US astronaut Neil Armstrong radioed back from the Moon to mission control in Houston, Texas, USA on 20 July 1969. The *Eagle* was the lunar module, which had detached from the spacecraft *Columbia*, in orbit 60 miles above the surface of the Moon. While astronaut Michael Collins remained on board *Columbia*, the Lunar Excursion Module touched down on an area called the Sea of Tranquility – but there is no water on the Moon so it didn't land with a splash! Neil Armstrong and Buzz Aldrin, the two astronauts inside the *Eagle*, became the first human beings ever to visit the Moon.

Astronaut Armstrong was the first to step out of the capsule onto the Moon (with his left foot). Buzz Aldrin followed him and looked around – at the totally black sky, the impact craters, the layers of moondust – and commented: 'Magnificent desolation.' As they'd been instructed, they quickly put moon rocks and dust into their pockets, so that they would have some samples of the Moon, even if they had to leave in a hurry.

In fact, they stayed for nearly a day on the Moon and covered nearly a kilometre on foot. This epic voyage of Apollo 11 remains one of the most inspirational journeys into the unknown that mankind has ever undertaken, and three craters to the north of the Sea of Tranquility are now named after the astronauts on the mission – Collins, Armstrong and Aldrin.

Walking on the Moon

Including Apollo 11, a total of 12 astronauts have now walked on the Moon. But each mission was still a dangerous business, as was clearly shown on the Apollo 13 mission in April 1970 when an explosion on board the service module meant that not only the astronauts but also the people on the ground had to make heroic efforts to return the spacecraft safely to Earth.

All the Apollo astronauts – including the ones from the harrowing 13 mission, came back safely. Astronauts are highly trained specialists with backgrounds in aviation, engineering and science. But to launch and operate a space mission needs people with a wide variety of skills. The Apollo missions – like all space missions before and since – were the result of work by tens of thousands of people who built and operated the complex hardware and software.

The Apollo missions also brought back 840lb of lunar material to be studied on Earth. This allowed scientists on our planet to gain a much better understanding of the Moon and how it relates to the Earth.

The last mission to the Moon was Apollo 17, which landed on the Taurus-Littrow highlands on 11 December 1972 and stayed for three days. When they were 29,000 kilometres from the Earth, the Apollo 17 crew took a photo of the complete Earth, fully lit. This photo is known as 'the Blue Marble' and may be the most widely distributed photo ever. Since then, no human being has been far enough away from the Earth to take such a picture.

The first man in space

The Apollo missions were not the first time that man had flown into space. Soviet cosmonaut Yuri Gagarin, who orbited the Earth on 12 April 1961 in the Vostok spacecraft, was the first-ever human being in space.

Six weeks after Gagarin's historic achievement, US President John F. Kennedy announced that he wanted to land a man on the Moon within ten years, and the newly created NASA – the National Aeronautics and Space Administration – set to work to see if they could match the Russian manned space programme, even though at that time, NASA had only 16 minutes of spaceflight experience. The space race – to be the first on the Moon – had begun!

Mercury, Gemini – and walking in space

Project Mercury, a US single-astronaut programme, was designed to see if human beings could survive in space. In 1961, astronaut Alan Shepard became the first American in space with a suborbital flight of fifteen minutes, and the following year, John Glenn became the first NASA astronaut to orbit the Earth.

NASA's Project Gemini followed. Gemini was a very important project as it taught astronauts how to dock vehicles in space. It also allowed them to practise operations such as space walks, also called EVAs (Extra Vehicular Activity). But the first space walk ever performed was by a Russian cosmonaut, Alexei Leonov, in 1965. The Russians didn't make it to the Moon, however, with this honour going to the USA in 1969.

The first space stations

After the race to land on the Moon was over, many people became less interested in space programmes. However, both the Russians and the Americans still had big plans. The Russians were working on a super-secret programme called Almaz – or Diamond. They wanted to have a manned space station orbiting the Earth. After a doomed first attempt, the next versions, Salyut-3 and then Salyut-5 were more successful but neither of them lasted for much more than a year.

The Americans developed their own version, Skylab – an orbiting space station which was in operation for eight months in 1973. Skylab had a telescope on board that astronauts used to observe the Sun. They brought back solar photographs including X-ray images of solar flares and dark spots on the Sun.

A handshake in space

At this time on Earth – the mid 1970s – both the USSR and the USA were locked into what was known as the Cold War. This meant the two sides were not actually fighting a war but they disliked and distrusted each other very strongly. However, in space the two countries began to work together. In 1975, the Apollo–Soyuz project saw the first 'hand-shake in space' between the two opposing superpowers. Apollo, the US spacecraft docked with Soyuz, the Soviet one, and the American astronaut and Russian cosmonaut – who would have had difficulty meeting in person on Earth – shook hands with each other.

The shuttle

The space shuttle was a new type of spacecraft. Unlike the craft that went before it, it was reusable, designed to fly into space like a rocket but also to glide back to Earth and land like an aeroplane, on a runway. The shuttle was also designed to take cargo as well as astronauts into space. The first US shuttle – *Columbia* – was launched in 1981.

The ISS

In 1986, the Russians launched space station Mir, which means World or Peace.

Mir was the first elaborate and large space station ever to orbit the Earth. It was built in space over ten years and designed as a 'space laboratory' so that scientists could carry out experiments in a nearly gravity-free environment. Mir was the size of six buses and was home to between three and six astronauts at a time.

The **International Space Station (ISS)** was built in space with its construction beginning in 1998. Orbiting the globe every 90 minutes, this research facility is a symbol of international co-operation with scientists and astronauts from many countries involved both in running it and spending time there. The ISS is serviced by the space shuttle from NASA, the Soyuz spacecraft from Russia and the European Space Agency's Automated Transfer Vehicles. The crew also have permanent escape vehicles, in case they need to make an emergency exit!

The future

In 2010, the space shuttle will go out of service and the ISS will receive supplies and crew from the Russian Soyuz and Progress spacecraft.

NASA is developing a new type of spacecraft, called Orion, which it hopes will take us back to the Moon and possibly beyond – to the red planet, Mars.

But a totally new type of space travel is also becoming a reality. In the future, 'space tourists' may be able to take short, suborbital flights. One day, perhaps, we will all be able to take holidays on the Moon!

The Agency had departments in several places in the USA, each one responsible for different aspects of space flight. Here in Florida, they ran the launch of space shuttles and robotic probes into the cosmos. In Houston, Texas, they took over control of the manned space flights once they had taken off, and in California there was a further mission control for the robotic space flights. Sometimes Eric went to visit these other offices, but he had decided to base his family in Florida so they wouldn't have to move around all the time.

Annie told the others that they had to get inside the main building at the Global Space Agency to collect their spacesuits, which Eric had stored there, so that, like the shuttle, they could leave the Earth and travel into space. They couldn't go without their suits because it would be too cold and they needed air to breathe and a way to communicate with Cosmos.

However, it was pretty much impossible for kids to get into the Global Space Agency by themselves: they not only had to have special passes but also a car to get there. Even though they had flown through space before, neither Annie nor George knew how to drive an ordinary Earth car so they needed Annie's dad to ferry them to the start point of their voyage of discovery. Obviously they weren't intending to tell Eric he was to be their cosmic taxi driver. They'd just let him think they were all going for a day out at the Global Space Agency: the master-plan they intended to put into action the minute he took his eyes off them was to remain a secret.

'When no one is looking—' continued Annie.

'What do you mean, *when no one is looking*?' interrupted George. 'I think your dad will notice if we suddenly disappear.'

'No he won't!' said Annie. 'He'll be too busy staring up at the spaceship in the sky. So that will be the moment I give the command for us to run. All we need to do is find the spacesuits, put them on, open up Cosmos and go through the doorway into space. It's simple, really,' she told them. 'The greatest plans always are. Just like Einstein said.'

'I think he was talking about scientific theories,' said George gently. 'Not kids travelling around the Solar System by themselves.'

'If Einstein was here now,' insisted Annie, 'he'd be saying, Annie Bellis, you are the coolest cat that ever wore pyjamas.'

Emmett's face had clouded over. 'Am I going into space?' he fretted. 'I mean, I really want to but I'm very allergic and I might—'

'No, Emmett,' said Annie. 'You are the controller of the cosmic journey. You're going to stay on Earth with

Cosmos and direct us. So you don't have to worry about meeting a peanut in space. It isn't going to happen.'

'Oh, phew,' said Emmett in relief. 'My mum would never forgive me.'

'And what are *we* going to do?' asked George.

'We,' said Annie, 'you and me, that is, are going to Mars. The truth is out there, George. And *we* are going to find it.'

Standing on a wide balcony high up on the Global Space Agency's main building, George, Annie and Emmett could see all the way across the swampland to where the space shuttle sat waiting, patiently and quietly, for take-off. Around it was the scaffolding that had been holding it upright – a steel cat's-cradle of joists and supports for the enormous spacecraft. Two railway lines led away from the launch pad to the largest building that George had ever seen.

'You see that place?' said Eric, pointing to the building. 'That's where they get the spaceship ready to send it into space. It's called the Vehicle Assembly Building and it's big enough to stand the spaceship up inside it. It's so tall that it has its own weather systems – sometimes clouds form inside.'

'You mean it can rain inside there?' said Annie.

'That's right,' Eric told her. 'You have to take an umbrella if you work in that building! When the Orbiter – that's the spacecraft part of the shuttle – is

ready to go, it leaves that building by rail and travels to the launch pad, where it's prepared for take-off.'

With its black-and-white nose pointing upwards, the Orbiter looked quite small against the giant orange fuel tank underneath it. On either side, the fuel tank was flanked by two long white rocket boosters, waiting for ignition.

'See, they've taken the arms of the scaffolding away now,' said Eric. 'That means they've closed all the hatches and the crew who've readied the shuttle for launch have left the area.'

'Just like on my computer game,' boasted Emmett, 'which teaches you how to fly the shuttle.'

'I'd like to try that,' said a voice behind him. George turned round. A woman in an all-in-one blue Global Space Agency suit stood behind him. George knew this outfit meant she was a real astronaut.

'OK!' said Emmett happily. 'I can let you do that. If you come over to our house this evening, I'll show you how it works.'

He caught Annie's eye. 'Or another day,' he added hastily. 'We're a bit busy right now and I might not have time. You could come over tomorrow, if you like. If we're back, that is. Not that we're going anywhere, but— Ouch!'

Annie had nudged him quite hard.

'I was just trying to be friendly!' he whispered to her. 'I thought you said that was a good thing to do!'

'I did!' she hissed back. 'But making friends with people doesn't mean you have to tell them everything we're up to the minute you meet them!'

'Then how do I make friends?' asked Emmett plaintively.

'Look, let's just get the planet saved, all right?' said Annie. 'And tomorrow I'll teach you about being friends with people and how it works? OK? Deal?'

'Deal,' said Emmett solemnly. 'This is turning out to be a mega-cool vacation.'

'But don't you know how to fly the space shuttle already?' said George, asking a question to deflect attention away from Emmett. 'Aren't you an astronaut?'

'Yes, that's right,' she said. 'I am an astronaut. I'm what's called a "Mission Specialist". That means I'm a scientist who goes up into space to perform experiments, do spacewalks and help build parts of the International Space Station. I am trained to fly spacecraft, but that isn't really my job. The Commander and the pilot fly the shuttle and dock it at the International

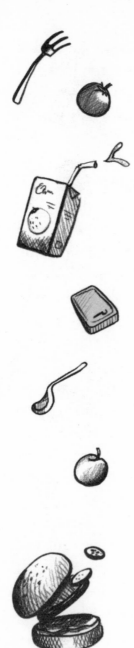

Space Station. When we get into the space station, that's when my work begins.'

'When you're in the space station,' said Annie, 'are you all just floating around?'

'We are,' said the astronaut. 'It's a lot of fun but it's quite difficult to do simple things like eat and drink. We have to drink through straws and our food comes in packets: we open them, dig our fork in and hope the food sticks to it and doesn't go flying around all over the place.'

'Do you ever have food fights?' asked George. 'That would be cool!'

'But how do you go to the toilet?' asked Emmett, looking perplexed. 'Isn't that very difficult in a low-gravity scenario?'

'Emmett!' squeaked Annie. 'I'm so sorry about him,' she said to the astronaut. 'He's really embarrassing.'

'Oh no!' The woman laughed. 'Don't be embarrassed about your brother's question.'

Annie's face was a picture of horror at the idea that anyone could think Emmett was her brother.

'Everyone asks about the space toilet,' said the astronaut. 'And yes, it is quite tricky at first. We have to do special training sessions to learn how.'

'You have toilet lessons to be an astronaut!' Emmett had turned pink with delight.

'It's just one of the things we have to learn to get by in space,' said the astronaut firmly. 'We train for several years learning the tasks we need to carry out during our two-week missions in space. We have to learn how to cope with being weightless and how to operate the shuttle's robotic arm and use all the other complicated electrical and mechanical equipment. Have any of you thought of becoming astronauts when you grow up?'

'I might do,' said Annie. 'It depends. You see, I want to be a physicist *and* a footballer so I might not have time for all that extra training.'

'What about you two?' the astronaut asked George and Emmett. 'Would you like to go into space?'

'Oh yes!' said George. 'I'd like that more than anything.'

Emmett shook his head. 'I have motion sickness.'

'We know,' said Annie. On the drive over, he had nearly been sick in her rucksack – the one with Cosmos in it. She'd had to snatch it away and push Emmett's head out of the car window to prevent a disaster. Even then, it hadn't been pleasant.

Eric appeared next to them, looking worried. 'Hello!' he said to the astronaut. 'I'm Eric – Eric Bellis from the Mars Science Laboratory.'

'The famous Eric!' she exclaimed. 'I'm Jenna. I've wanted to meet you for ages. It's great, the work you're doing on life in the Universe. We're all very excited about Homer and what he might find on Mars. We can't wait to hear the results!'

'Ah, well . . .' Eric frowned. 'Um, yes, we're . . . excited too.' But he didn't sound it. 'I see you've met the kids.' He was fidgeting with his pager, which let him know if anything important was happening, either on the Earth or on Mars.

'I have!' said Jenna. 'Are they all yours?'

'Er, no,' said Eric. 'Just Annie, the blonde one. The rest I seem to have collected somehow.' But he smiled as he spoke. 'These are her friends, George and Emmett.' His pager suddenly beeped furiously in his hand. 'Oh, collapsing stars!' he said to himself and looked up. 'I've been sent an urgent alert,' he told Jenna. 'I've got to get to the control room immediately.'

'You can leave the kids with me,' she said. 'I'm sure nothing will happen to them.' They shuffled their feet and looked rather guilty. 'You can page me when you're done,' she continued cheerfully. 'I'll let you know where to collect them.'

'Thank you,' said Eric, and shot off down the stairs. As he left, the clock on the wall that displayed the time to take-off had started moving again. From time to time it stopped in order to allow more checks – of everything, from the shuttle launch systems, to the computers on the Orbiter, to the weather in different locations around the world – to take place. Once all the checks were completed and everyone was happy, the clock moved on again. This time they were just seconds away from lift-off. George gripped Annie's hand as everyone called out to count down the final seconds together.

'Five . . . four . . . three . . . two . . . *one*!'

The first thing they saw was a great cloud of dust at the bottom of the spaceship, billowing outwards in slow, soft, pillowy folds of greyish white. As the spacecraft rose up from the ground, George and Annie could see a brilliant light under the tail. The spaceship moved upwards as though pulled by an invisible thread, the light beneath it so bright it was like seeing the skies ripped open to reveal an angel or some other celestial being appear from within. The spaceship climbed higher and higher, the mighty blast beneath it sending it vertically into the heavens.

'It's so quiet,' whispered George to Annie. 'It's

not making any noise.'

Until that moment, the spaceship seemed to be starting its cosmic journey in complete silence, as though they were watching it on television with the sound turned off. But seconds later, the noise rolled over the intervening miles towards them. First they heard a strange crackling sound; then the full force of the boom hit them – the sound seemed to swallow them whole. It was so loud, it blocked out everything else. They felt a pounding in their chests so intense that they thought they might be knocked backwards by the wave of sound.

HOW SOUND TRAVELS THROUGH SPACE

On Earth there are lots of atoms close together and knocking each other around. Giving atoms a kick can make them kick their neighbouring atoms, and then those atoms kick other atoms, and so on, so the kick travels through the mass of atoms. Lots of little kicks can create a stream of vibrations travelling through a material. The air covering the Earth's surface consists of a large number of gas atoms and molecules bouncing off each other; it can carry vibrations like this, as can the sea, the rock beneath our feet and even everyday objects. The vibrations that are the right sort to stimulate our ears we call sound.

It takes time for sound to travel through a material because an atom has to pass each kick on to its neighbours. How much time depends on how strongly the atoms affect each other, which depends on the nature of the material and other things like the temperature. In air, sound travels at around one mile every five seconds. This is about one million times slower than the speed of light, which is why the light from a space shuttle launch is seen almost immediately by the spectators, while the noise arrives a bit later. In the same way a lightning flash arrives before the thunder – which is the kick given to the air molecules by the sudden and intense electrical discharge. In the sea, sound travels at around five times faster than it does in air.

In outer space it is very different. Between stars atoms are very rare, so there is nothing to kick against. Of course, if you have air in your spacecraft, sound inside it will travel normally. A small rock hitting the outside will make the wall of the craft vibrate, and then the air inside, so you might hear that. But sounds created on a planet, or in another spacecraft, would not carry to you unless someone there converted them into radio waves (which are like light and don't need a material to carry them), and you used your radio receiver to convert them back into sound inside your ship.

There are also natural radio waves travelling through space, produced by stars and faraway galaxies. Radio astronomers examine these in the same way that other astronomers examine visible light from space. Because radio waves are not visible, and we are used to converting them into sound using radio receivers, radio astronomy is sometimes thought of as 'listening', rather than 'looking'. But both radio and visible-light astronomers are doing the same thing: studying types of electromagnetic waves from space. There isn't really any sound from space at all.

The roar of the engines rang through their whole bodies as the spaceship curved away, leaving a trail of white smoke behind it. As they stood and watched it climb ever upwards, they saw the wispy white clouds form into a shape against the blue sky.

'That looks like a heart,' said Annie dreamily. 'Like it's saying: *From the space shuttle with love.*' But a second later, she shook herself back into action again. Looking around, she saw that all the adults were still gazing up at the sky. She grabbed George and Emmett.

'OK, I'll give the countdown,' she said, 'and then we run! Are you ready? Five, four, three, two, *one* . . .'

Chapter 8

As the spaceship disappeared into the skies above, the kids also vanished – down the same stairway Eric had taken. They found themselves inside a huge building with long corridors leading in all directions.

'I think it's this way,' said Annie, but she didn't sound at all sure. They rushed down the hallway after her, past framed pictures of astronauts and drawings done by the children of astronauts, which hung on the wall to commemorate each mission.

'Um, let's try this door.' Annie pushed hard and they burst into a huge room full of giant pieces of machinery.

'Oops!' she said, backing out rapidly, treading on George and Emmett behind her. 'Not that door, then.'

'Do you actually know where you're going?' asked George.

'Of course I do!' said Annie huffily. 'I just got a bit confused because all these places look a bit the same. We need the Clean Room. That's where they keep the suits. Let's go this way.'

George's heart sank at the idea of Annie navigating her way around the Solar System. If she couldn't find her way around the Global Space Agency, which she claimed to have visited many times, could she really be trusted to take them to Mars and back?

But Annie was not to be deterred. She dragged them along to another door, which she shoved open. The room was in darkness, apart from an illuminated screen at the front, where a man was pointing to a picture of Saturn.

'And so we can see that the rings of Saturn,' he was saying, 'are made up of dust and rocks in orbit around the giant gas planet.'

George thought back to the little rock from Saturn he had once pocketed when he and Annie were riding around the Solar System on a comet. Unfortunately a teacher at George's school had thought the precious rock was nothing more than a handful of dust and had made George throw it in the bin. *If only!* he thought. If only he'd been able to bring that little rock here. What clues about the Universe might they have been able to discover from his fragment of Saturn?

They came to a door marked COMETS, but it was locked.

'*Ping-pong!*' they heard from inside the rucksack on Annie's back. Cosmos seemed to have switched himself on.

'Cosmos!' said George. 'You must stay quiet! We're trying to find the Clean Room and we don't want anyone to notice us.'

'Do I sound like I'm bovvered?' came the reply. 'Do I? Do I?'

'Oh, shush!' said George urgently.

'*D'you wanna dance wiv me?*' sang Cosmos tunelessly.

'Of course not, you're a computer,' said George. 'Why would I want to do that?'

'Are ya feelin' me!'

'Emmett, make him be quiet!' ordered Annie.

'Actually,' said Emmett, 'it would be better to leave him switched on right now – if I close him down and then have to open him up quickly, we might have even more problems.'

'Over there!' said George, spotting a sign on a huge pair of double doors. It read CLEAN ROOM. 'Is that where the suits are?'

'That's it!' said Annie. 'I remember it now. I've never been inside but it's where they keep all the equipment that goes into space. It's a super-duper clean environment so that bugs and stuff don't go from Earth into space.'

'Oh yes,' said Emmett nerdily. 'It's very important that microbes don't travel into space with any of the machinery. Otherwise how would we ever know if we've found evidence of life in space or whether we're just seeing fingerprints that we ourselves left out there?'

Annie ran over to the double doors. 'Follow me!' she said. 'Most of the people should be upstairs, watching the launch.'

They went through, expecting to emerge in the Clean Room, but there was a surprise in store for them. They found themselves standing on a moving conveyor belt. Gusts of air started blowing at them from all sides as the belt dragged them along. Brushes emerged from the ceiling as they were sprayed with jets and buffed with a huge piece of fabric.

'What's happening?' shouted George.

'We're being *cleaned*!' Annie called back.

'Arrghh!' shouted Cosmos. 'They're messin' wiv ma ports!'

In front of him, George saw a pair of robotic arms pick Annie up and drop her into an all-in-one white

plastic suit, pop a hat on her head, a mask on her face and a pair of gloves on her hands. Before he had time to call out, she was ejected from the conveyor belt through another set of double doors and it was his turn. George and then Emmett behind him were similarly kitted out by the machine and propelled through the doorway, where they stood, blinking at the incredible whiteness that surrounded them.

It was, thought George, like being inside someone's very white set of teeth. On one side of them was a robot under construction; on the other, what looked like half a satellite. Everything seemed to gleam with an unusual brightness. Even the air felt somehow thinner and more

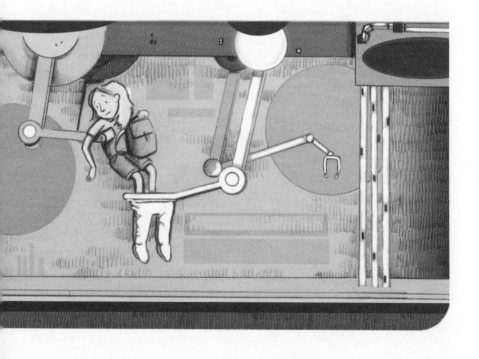

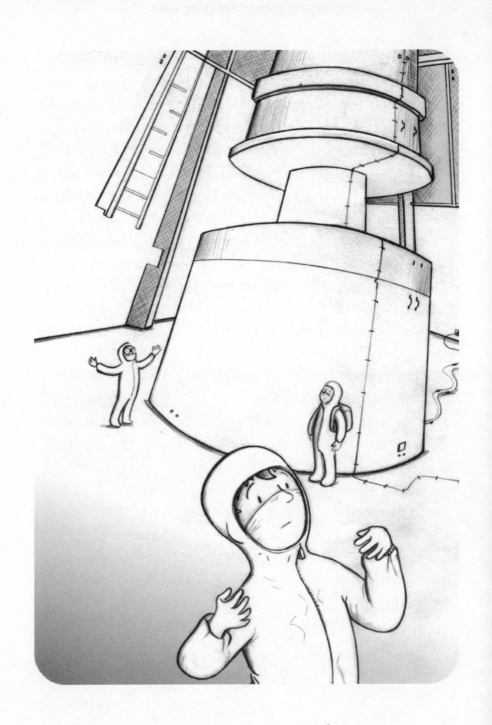

transparent than normal air. On the wall, a sign read: 100,000.

'That's how many particles the air has in here,' whispered Emmett through his face mask. 'This isn't the cleanest clean room – in there, they have a 10,000 rating – that means any cubic foot of air in there has no more than 10,000 particles in it larger than half a micron! And a micron is a millionth of a metre.'

'Is it clean enough for us to go to Mars from here?' asked George. 'I mean, what if we take some evidence of life on Earth to Mars and then Homer finds it later on? Could we mess up the research programme?'

'Theoretically, yes,' said Emmett, who was sounding much more confident, now that he felt they'd entered his area of expertise. 'But that rather depends on a) whether we can get Cosmos working; b) whether you actually manage to get to Mars; and c) whether Annie's alien message really *is* a threat to destroy the Earth. If she's right – and I have to point out the probability is very low – then if you don't go, there won't be life on Earth anyway. So it won't matter.'

In a corner of the Clean Room, Annie had found some spacesuits, but they were bright orange and didn't look at all like the ones George remembered from his travels around the Universe in the past.

'These aren't ours!' Annie said in disappointment. 'These are the ones they use for the space shuttle – they're different from the ones me and my dad had.'

She rootled around a bit further. 'Dad told me he'd put ours in here for safekeeping,' she said. 'And I said, what if someone else took them by mistake? And he said they wouldn't because he'd labelled them as prototype suits, not to be used for shuttle missions.'

Emmett was tearing at the plastic wrapping that the Clean Room entry machinery had used to cover Annie's rucksack. He fished Cosmos out – and at the same time found the bright yellow book: *The User's Guide to the Universe.*

'OK, little 'puter,' he said, flexing his fingers. 'Operation Alien Life Form is underway. Where to, Commander George?'

'See if you can get him to open the doorway,' said George. 'We need to go to Mars – to the north polar region, destination Homer.'

'Bingo!' shouted Annie. 'I've got the suits!' She emerged with an armful of white spacesuits in plastic coverings marked PROTOTYPE – DO NOT USE! She chucked one over to George. 'Take off your face mask and then put this on over everything else.' She and George ripped the coverings off the suits and started clambering into the heavy space gear.

Meanwhile Emmett had called up some pictures of Mars on Cosmos's screen, zooming closer and closer to the red planet. However, Cosmos himself was being unusually silent.

'Why is he so quiet?' asked George.

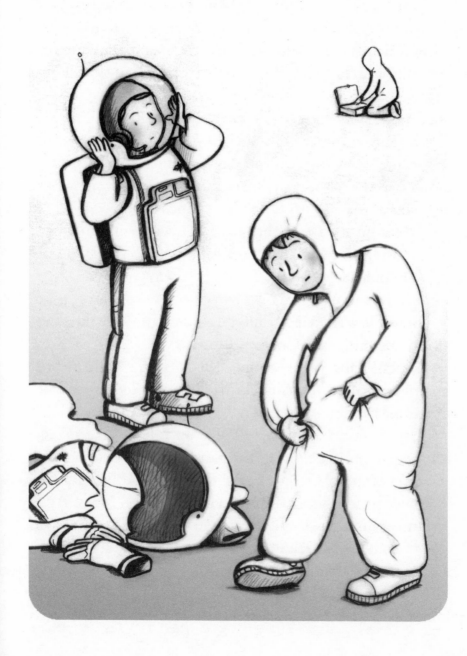

'I had a brilliant idea,' said Emmett simply. 'I turned down the volume.'

He turned it up and they heard Cosmos grumbling, 'Nobody cares about me. No one understands me. No one wants to know how I feel.'

Emmett turned it down again.

'We'll need to be able to talk to Cosmos when we're out there,' warned Annie. 'We got stuck in space once, and once was enough. Can you handle him?'

Emmett turned up the volume once more.

'*Do this, do that,* that's all I ever hear,' moaned Cosmos. 'I just wanna express myself.'

'Cosmos,' said Annie, 'I've got a way you can show us how you feel.'

'Bet you want me to open up a doorway so you can go through it,' said Cosmos morosely.

'That's right,' said George, 'but the thing is, we're not really allowed to do this. So we'll be in a lot of trouble if we get caught.'

'Cool!' said Cosmos, perking up a bit. 'You mean, this would be, like, a seriously dred thing to do?'

'Er, yes,' said George, 'but we need you to help us. We need you to look after us while we're on Mars. And you too, Emmett. If we need to leave quickly, you have to get us out of there immediately.'

'But,' said Emmett, 'if you signal me from Mars, then won't there be a time delay? I mean, it takes four minutes and twenty seconds for light to travel from

Mars. Or, if Mars is on the other side of the Sun, it could be twenty-two minutes. So by the time you've said something to me and I've replied, it will have taken either eight minutes and forty seconds or forty-four minutes. And that might be too late.'

'No, Cosmos has Instant Messaging,' said Annie. 'So you'll hear us and reply immediately.'

'Wow! That's some pretty special physics!' said Emmett, looking impressed.

'That is,' Annie added, 'if Cosmos isn't too chicken to do this—'

'Safe! I'm on it!' said Cosmos. A little beam of white light shot out from the great computer: in the middle of the Clean Room, the kids saw the shape of a doorway emerge.

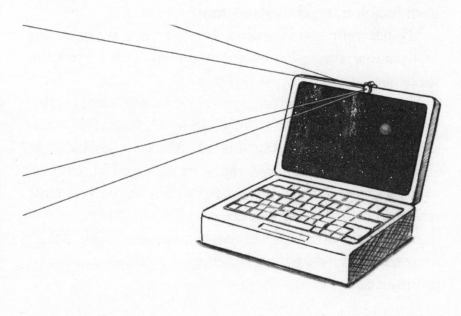

The door swung open. Behind it, they saw a reddish planet coming into view. There was a large dark patch on its middle left-hand side.

'Approaching Mars,' said Emmett as the planet drew closer, stars shining brightly in the black sky behind it. 'See that dark spot? That's Syrtis Major. That's a huge area of dark, windswept volcanic plain so large it has been known to science since the first telescope was turned to Mars in the 1600s. The southern polar ice cap is large and visible at this time of year. The bright feature at the lower centre is the Hellas Basin, the largest undisputed impact crater on the planet, formed by an asteroid or comet. It is 1,370 miles across. Those four points you see in the equatorial region – they're clouds of water ice crystals over the four largest volcanoes in Tharsis.'

'How do you know all this?' said George, speaking in a strange voice through the voice transmitter in the space helmet he had just put on.

'Actually, I'm getting it from Cosmos's screen,' said Emmett almost apologetically. 'He's giving me a readout of the conditions on Mars to check it is safe for you to land. On the way, he's giving a bit of tourist advice. It says here that visitors to Mars should remember that gravitational conditions there will be quite different from what you're used to. You'll weigh under half of what you weigh on Earth, so get ready to bounce.'

'Does he say what the weather is like?' said Annie through her voice transmitter. She sounded rather nervous.

'Let's look . . .' said Emmett. 'Here's today's forecast for the north polar region of Mars: *Today will be mostly clear with an average temperature of minus sixty Celsius. Possibility of water ice storms in the area: very low. But dust storms could start from the central region and engulf the planet.* I'd better keep an eye on that. It says here that dust storms are common at this time of year and can spread very fast.'

The doorway got closer and closer to Mars, breaking through the thin atmosphere and heading down towards the rocky surface.

George and Annie stood on the threshold, holding hands in their big space gloves, their oxygen tanks plugged in and their transmission devices switched on. As they hovered a few metres above the ground, Annie said, 'Are you ready? Five, four, three, two, one . . . *jump*!'

They disappeared through the doorway and found themselves on Mars – a planet where no human being had ever set foot before.

Emmett saw them vanish; then a spray of red Martian dust floated through the portal before the door slammed shut.

He tried to capture some of the dust as it drifted through the super-clean air but it was quickly sucked away through the many filters in the Clean Room, designed to dispose of any pollution immediately. Like Annie and George, the Martian dust disappeared completely, leaving Emmett alone with Cosmos in the huge room. He gazed around for a few minutes and then picked up *The User's Guide to the Universe*.

He looked up Mars in the index and turned to the right page.

'*Did Life Come From Mars?*' he read.

DID LIFE COME FROM MARS?

Where and when did life as we know it begin? Did it begin on Earth? Or could it have come from Mars?

A couple of centuries ago, most people believed that humans, and other species, had been present since the creation of the Earth. The Earth was thought to be, essentially, the whole of the material world, and the creation was described as a rather sudden event, like the Big Bang that the majority of scientists believe in today. This was taught in creation stories, like the one in Genesis, the first book of the Bible, and other cultures throughout the world have similar stories of a one-off moment of creation.

Although some astronomers did think about the vastness of space, its study only really began after Galileo (1564–1642) made one of the first ever telescopes; his discoveries showed that the Universe contained many other worlds – some of which could, like our own planet, be inhabited. The immensity of the Universe – and the evidence that its creation must have happened *long before* the arrival on the scene of our own species – did not begin to be generally recognized until much later on, in what is known as the Age of Enlightenment. This was the eighteenth-century period in which there were many inventions, such as the hydrogen balloon, and particularly the steam engine. These inventions triggered the technological and industrial revolution of the following (nineteenth) century. During that innovative time, the study of rock formation by sedimentation in shallow seas led geologists to understand that such processes must have been going on, not just for thousands or even millions of years, but for thousands of millions of years – what we now call giga-years.

Modern geophysicists now believe our planet Earth – and our Solar System – was formed about 4.6 giga-years ago, when the Universe – now aged about 14 giga-years – was itself just over 9 giga-years old.

Modern humans appear to have arrived in the rest of the world from Africa 50,000 years ago, but modern archaeology has shown quite clearly that it was only about 6,000 years ago that early human societies began to develop what we call civilization – economic systems with the exchange of different kinds of goods. A very important factor in any civilization is the exchange not just of goods but of *information*. But how was this information stored or spread? Suitable recording mechanisms were needed.

Before the invention of paper and ink, one of the earliest methods was to use marks scratched on clay tablets – the distant ancestors of modern computer memory chips. This sharing and collection of knowledge, particularly the kind we now call scientific, became an objective in its own right.

The (relatively recent) development of civilization depended, of course, on the emergence of what has been called *intelligent life*: beings with a sufficient sense of self-awareness to recognize themselves in a mirror. There are several known examples on our own planet: elephants, dolphins, and of course anthropoids – the group that includes chimpanzees and other apes, Neanderthals, and modern human beings like us. So far no signs of intelligent life have been detected elsewhere in the Universe.

How did these intelligent life forms on Earth come into being? Fossil remains had suggested the idea that modern plants and animals could have arisen from other life forms present on Earth in earlier times, but people couldn't understand how the various species could be so well adapted without being having been designed in advance. The idea of continuous evolution became generally accepted only after Darwin (in 1859) explained the principle of adaptation by *natural selection*. Understanding how this actually works, however, only became possible much more recently (in the late 1950s), when Watson and Crick made their discoveries about DNA.

This modern DNA-based understanding of the evolutionary process is supported by the fossil record – as far as it goes. The trouble is that the record does not go very far back – less than a giga-year, which is only a fraction of the total age of the Earth.

Early, simple life forms developed before what is known as the Cambrian era. We can see fairly clearly how (though not precisely why) what we should recognize as intelligent life forms evolved from them over the last 500 million years. But there is no proper record of how the pre-Cambrian life forms evolved in the first place.

One problem is that it is only since the Cambrian era that large bony animals, which turn easily into fossils, have been present. Their largest predecessors are believed to be soft-bodied creatures (like modern jellyfish); further back in time the only life forms seem to have been microscopic single-celled creatures. These don't leave clear fossil records.

Going back even further, it is evident that evolution must have been very slow. And tricky to achieve. Even if environmentally favourable planets were fairly common in the Universe, the odds against the evolution of advanced life on any single planet would have been very high. This means that it would occur on only a very small fraction of them. The planet on which we find ourselves must be one of those rare exceptions. And it could still have easily gone wrong. There is a calculation by astrophysicists known as the *solar age coincidence*. This shows that, in the time taken by evolution on Earth to lead to intelligent life, a large part of the hydrogen fuel reserves powering our Sun were used up. In a nutshell, if our evolution had been just a little bit slower we would never have got here at all before the Sun burned itself out!

So which of the essential evolutionary steps would be the hardest to achieve in the available time?

One difficult step on Earth may have been the beginning of what is known as *eukaryotic life* – in which cells have an elaborate structure with nuclei and ribosomes. Eukaryotes include large, multi-cellular animals like us, as well as single-celled species like the amoeba. The fossil record shows that the first eukaryotic life appeared on Earth at the beginning of the Proterozoic aeon, about two giga-years ago, when the Earth was only about half its present age. Before this period, more primitive *procaryotic* life forms, such as bacteria (with cells that are too small to contain nuclei), are now thought to have been widespread. This was in what is known as the Archaean aeon, which began when the Earth was less than one giga-year old.

There is evidence for the existence of this kind of primitive life right back at the very beginning of this aeon – so we are now faced with a puzzle, because this implies that the whole process by which life actually originated must have occurred during the *preceding* epoch. This is known as the Hadean aeon – the earliest aeon of the Earth's history.

Why should this be a problem? Well, the Hadean aeon was certainly long enough – nearly a giga-year – but conditions on Earth at that time would have been literally infernal, as the name suggests ('Hades' is the ancient Greek version of hell). This was when debris left over from the formation of the Solar System was crashing into the Moon and forming craters there. And the Earth – with its greater mass and gravitational attraction – would at that time have been subject to even heavier cratering. This bombardment would have caused frequent reheating of our planetary environment. Incipient life forms could hardly have avoided being nipped in the bud.

The planet Mars, however, has a lesser mass and is further away from the Sun, so it has recently been proposed that the bombardment of Mars could have subsided sooner than that of the Earth. Chunks of debris may also have been frequently knocked off Mars and in some cases subsequently swept up by the Earth.

This would mean that life may have originated on Mars – before it could have survived here.

Analysis by electron microscope of a meteorite that did reach Earth from Mars (meteorite ALH8400) has shown structures resembling fossil microbes. This proves that *fossil* organisms may have reached the Earth from Mars. But that would still not account for *life* then appearing here unless *living* – not just fossil – organisms could survive the necessary migration by meteor. This is a question that is currently being very hotly debated.

An even more interesting question is whether the environment on Mars at that time (in what is known as the Phyllocian period, roughly coinciding with the Hadean era on the Earth) really would have been suitable for primitive life.

Conditions on Mars nowadays are clearly unfavourable, at least on the surface – a cold dry desert with hardly any atmosphere except for a little carbon dioxide. Probes landing on Mars have, however, confirmed that there is a considerable amount of frozen water at the poles. Additionally, there are many observable features of the kind expected from erosion by rivers or by surf at a seashore. This means that at some stage in the Martian past there must have been a large amount of liquid water present – exactly what is needed for our kind of life to begin. During that early period the water would have formed an ocean. Initially this could have been several thousand metres deep with its centre near what is now the Martian north pole.

So life could have originated at the edge of this ocean, way back in Martian history.

There are a couple of objections to this theory. One is that the atmosphere would not have contained oxygen. However, primitive life forms on Earth are believed to have been been able to survive in an atmosphere that was also very deficient in oxygen so that might not have mattered.

Another objection is that the ancient Martian ocean would have been too salty for known terrestrial life forms. But maybe Martian life was originally adapted to very salty conditions, or perhaps it developed in freshwater lakes?

Thus life may well have begun on Mars – at the edge of a huge ocean there – then hitched a ride to the Earth on board a meteor. So our ultimate ancestors may, in fact, have been Martians!

Brandon

Chapter 9

As George and Annie jumped through the portal doorway, George twisted round to look back. For a millisecond he saw the Clean Room on planet Earth, and Emmett's worried face peering through the portal.

But then the doorway closed and disappeared entirely, leaving no trace in the dusty Martian sky of where it had once been.

Propelled by the force of their leap through the doorway, George and Annie travelled through the Martian atmosphere without landing for a few metres. They were holding hands tightly so they didn't lose each other on this strange and empty planet. George touched down but the impact of his feet on the surface sent them back up again in a great bouncing leap.

'Where are the mountains?' he called to Annie through the transmitter as they landed again and quickly dropped the other one's hand. They were standing on a huge expanse of flat, rubble-strewn, reddish ground. As far as they could see on either side, there was nothing but an endless scattering of red rocks across the desert planet. In the sky, the Sun – the same star that shone so brightly on the Earth – seemed more distant, smaller and colder, its light and warmth coming from farther away than on their home planet. The light looked pink because of all the red dust floating in the air, but it wasn't the beautiful familiar rosy glow of an earthly sunrise. Instead, it was a luminous colour that seemed alien and unwelcoming to the first humanoids ever to complete the long journey from Earth to Mars.

'No mountains here,' Annie told George. 'We're at the north pole of Mars. The volcanoes and valleys are in the middle of the planet.'

'How long have we got until sunset?' he asked, suddenly realizing they wouldn't be able to see anything once the Sun went down. The absolute nothingness of this empty planet was giving him the creeps and he certainly didn't want to be there in the dark.

'Ages,' said Annie. 'The sun doesn't set at the north pole in summer. But I don't want to stay that long. I don't like it here.' Even though her spacesuit protected her from the conditions on Mars, she shivered.

It wasn't nice to be so lonely and, like George, Annie suddenly missed being on a planet with people, buildings, movement, noise and life. Even though they sometimes felt they would love to live on a planet where there was no one to annoy them or order them around, the reality was very different. On an empty planet, there would be nothing to do and no one to play with. They might have dreamed of being masters of their very own world, but when it came down to it, home didn't seem so bad after all.

George jumped into the air again, to see how high he could go. He rose about a couple of feet and landed a second later, not far from where Annie was still standing.

'That was amazing!' he said.

Together, they drifted down towards the Martian surface, but once again, as soon as they touched down, they took off again.

'We'd better try not to leave too many footprints,' warned Annie, pointing to the marks George had made on the surface, 'or people will see them when the Mars Orbiter passes over this place and takes a photo. And then they'll think there really are Martians.'

'I can see Homer!' said George, spotting a lonely little figure in the distance. Separately now, they bounced closer. 'But what's he doing?' he added in amazement. The robot looked very busy. He was rolling to and fro, chucking bits of rock in the air.

'That's what we're here to find out,' said Annie. 'I'm going to call Emmett. Emmett!' she said into her voice transmitter. 'Emmett? Bother! He's not answering.'

They took a few long paces towards Homer and watched as he trundled mysteriously – but purposefully – about.

'Keep down!' hissed Annie, crouching. 'Otherwise Homer might see us through his camera eyes. And

then my dad will spot us on Mars and he'll know where we are. That would be a disaster!'

'But he won't see us for a few minutes,' said George. 'Not until the signal gets back to Earth. So even if Homer does take a picture of us, we'd still have time to get away.'

'Huh!' Annie snorted. 'It's OK for you. If my dad sees us here, all that will happen to you is he'll send you straight back to England. But I'll be stuck here – well, not here exactly. Not on Mars, but on Earth, with him being angry with me. And with every kind of boring punishment he can think of.'

'Like what?' asked George.

'Oh, I don't know!' said Annie. 'No football and extra maths homework and washing spacesuits and no pocket money for ever and ever and ever, I expect. Honestly, planet Earth won't feel big enough.'

'Do we have to be quiet as well? Can Homer hear us?' asked George.

'Hmm, don't think so,' said Annie. 'Mars has the wrong sort of atmosphere for noise to travel, so I don't think he's recording any sound, just pictures.' She paused for a second and then shouted into her voice transmitter, 'BUT I WISH EMMETT COULD HEAR US!'

'Ouch!' said George, whose space helmet felt like it might explode from the sound of Annie's voice erupting into it.

'Who? What? Where?' Finally they heard Emmett.

'Emmett, you twit!' said Annie. 'Why didn't you answer before?'

'Sorry,' came Emmett's voice. 'I was just reading something . . . Are you OK?'

'Yes, we are, no thanks to you, ground control,' said Annie. 'We have landed on Mars and we are approaching Homer. Do you have any further information for us?'

'Just checking,' murmured Emmett. 'I'll get back to you.'

'Can I boing right over him?' asked George longingly. He was really enjoying the lower gravity on Mars and wanted to keep jumping higher and higher. 'Then I could look down to see what he's doing?' George's white spacesuit had turned reddish brown from the Martian dust.'

'No, you'd crash into him!' said Annie. 'You can only go about two and a half times higher on Mars than you can on Earth. So don't try anything silly. We need to get to Homer,' she said, 'but stay to one side. That way we should miss the camera as well.'

They took a few giant loopy steps nearer to the robot, who was now motionless after his burst of frenzied activity, as though it had worn him out and he needed a rest.

'He's stopped messing round. Let's creep up on him!' said Annie. It wasn't easy to tiptoe in heavy space boots but they did their best to approach the robot without him noticing. As they sneaked up on Homer they saw the robot with his legs splayed firmly against the Martian ground, his dusty solar arrays – the panels that allowed him to collect radiation from the Sun and turn it into energy – his thick rubber wheels, his camera with the beady flashing eyes and the long robotic arm that now hung limply by his side.

But as they got near to him, they noticed something else – something they hadn't seen on the pictures Homer had sent back from Mars.

'Over there!' said Annie. 'Look!'

Next to Homer on the flat Martian surface they saw a series of marks made in the dust and rubble by Homer's tyres.

'It's a message!' yelled George, forgetting not to shout while wearing the voice transmitter. 'It's just like the one Cosmos received! It's the same sort of marks! Someone has left us a message on Mars!'

Annie kicked him with her space boot. 'Don't shout!' she whispered.

At the same time they heard Emmett's excited voice from planet Earth. 'A message? On Mars? What does it say?'

'We're trying to work it out,' said Annie. 'What if Homer wasn't just messing around – what if all that dancing around he did was because he was writing a message for us?'

They took a careful stride which landed them right next to the squiggles Homer had drawn on in the dust.

'It's going to take a few goes,' he warned, 'before I can work it out.'

He and Annie bounced together back and forth over the message as they tried to make sense of it.

'Can you tell me anything about the marks?' asked Emmett urgently. 'Anything I can enter to see what Cosmos makes of it?'

Just then George and Annie were flying right over the message. 'Um, well,' said George, 'there's a circle surrounded by other circles.'

'It could be a planet with rings,' said Annie. 'It could be Saturn. And look, next to it, all those rocks arranged in a row, that could be the Solar

System, like in the other message.'

'And over there – there's the planet with rings again but it's also got lots of little bits of stone arranged around it.'

'Maybe it's the moons of Saturn,' came Emmett's voice. 'Do you think the message wants you to go to the moons of Saturn? I'm putting the information into Cosmos now, to see if he can give us another clue. Can you count how many little bits of stone? Saturn has quite a lot – about sixty. But only seven round ones.'

The wind, which had been just a breeze, was now starting to blow more strongly, whipping bits of surface rubble up into the air and whirling them around.

'Oh no! Severe weather warning' – Emmett read off Cosmos's screen – 'incoming gales from the south. Potential evacuation situation.'

'We need more time!' George replied. 'We don't know what the message means yet! We're trying to count the moons around the planet with rings.'

'But it does have the same ending,' pointed out Annie, whose blood had run colder than space itself when she saw the last picture in the row. 'It still says no planet Earth.' They made another jump and landed right next to Homer. Annie got hold of his legs with her hand to stop herself from falling over in the strong wind; with the other hand, she grabbed onto George.

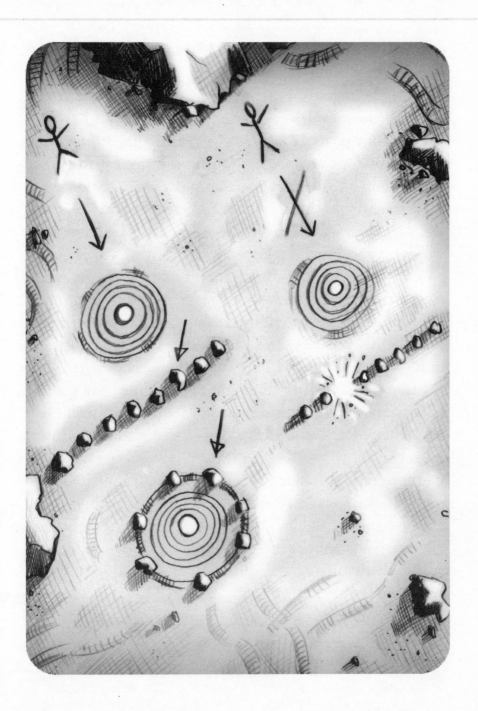

Emmett came back over the transmitter, sounding panicked. 'I don't think you *have* more time,' he said urgently. 'Cosmos has detected a giant dust storm, which is spreading very fast towards you! We have to get you out of there before you get lost in it! Cosmos says he may not be able to find you in a dust storm— Oh!' He broke off abruptly.

'Emmett, what is it?' Annie and George had just seen the huge dust clouds in the far distance, rolling over the empty ground towards them.

'Cosmos is stalled!' Emmett said in despair. 'He says: *Reverse portal not available at this moment due to an urgent system update.* Until he's finished updating, he can't bring you back! He can only send you further out!'

'Em, get us out of here!' shouted Annie, not caring how much noise she made now. 'Send us somewhere! Anywhere! But out of this storm! I can't hold on much longer!'

The wind was blowing the surface dust up around them. Homer was already covered in it, his shiny solar arrays blanked out. George and Annie could only just see each other as the torrent swirled around them. Annie was still hanging

onto Homer's leg, with George floating out behind her, buffeted by the terrible winds. He had both hands held tightly around one of Annie's arms. But they both knew that, at any second, they could be blown away from each other and lost for ever on Mars.

'The moons of Saturn!' yelled George into his voice transmitter. 'If you can't bring us back, send us further out! Send us to the next clue!'

Through the gritty cloud, which was growing thicker by the second, they saw the faint outline of a doorway standing right next to them. As it became more solid-looking, George let go of Annie with one arm and grabbed the doorframe. Swivelling round, he braced his feet against it, still holding tightly onto Annie, who was in turn still attached to Homer.

'Open the door!' he bellowed to Emmett on Earth. 'Annie! When I count down, I'm going to throw you through it! Let go of Homer!'

'I can't!' screamed Annie. 'I can't let go!'

George realized she was frozen with fear that she might be blown away if she released her hold on Homer.

'You have to!' he shouted back. 'I can't pull you *and* Homer through the doorway! I'm not strong enough!'

The door swung open very fast. Behind it they could see a mysterious orange swirl.

'On my count, Annie, let go!' said George. 'Five, four, three, two, *one*.' He tried to hurl her through the door

Sir Isaac Newton's own drawing of his reflecting telescope.

Dome of the Isaac Newton Telescope, La Palma.

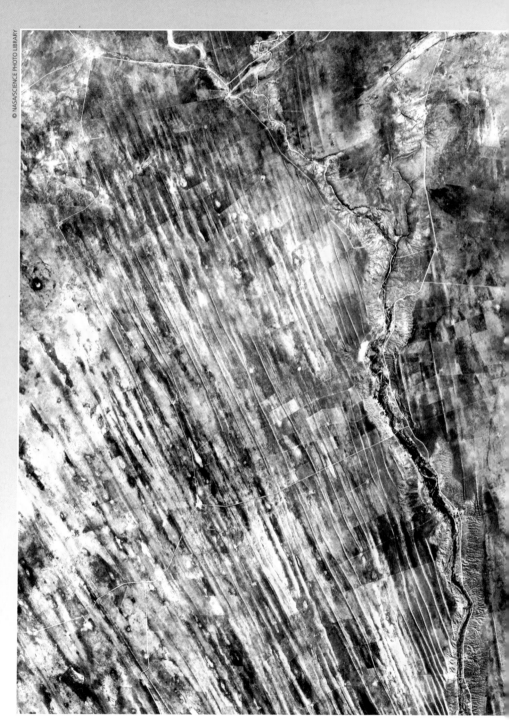

Kalahari Desert, Namibia, as seen from Space.

Leonid meteor shower.

Earth view of the planet Venus with the Moon.

Deployment of the Hubble Space telescope from the space shuttle Discovery, 1990.

Coloured optical image of the Rosette nebula.

Optical image of the Tarantula nebula.

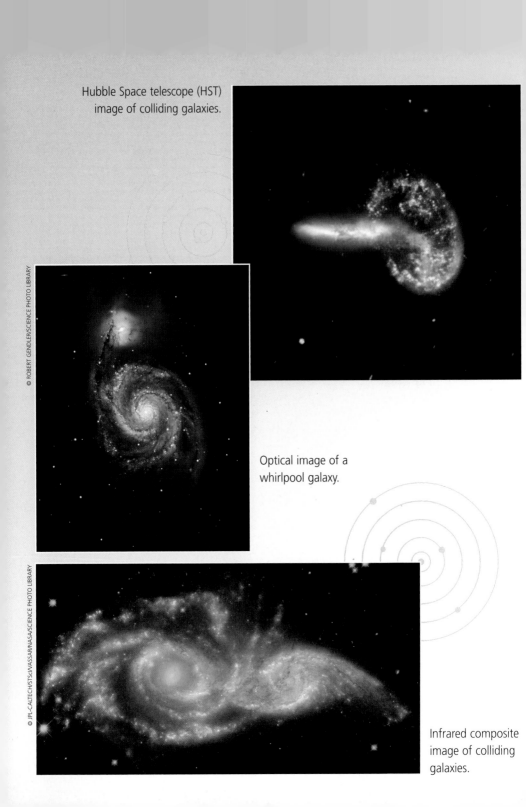

Hubble Space telescope (HST) image of colliding galaxies.

© ROBERT GENDLER/SCIENCE PHOTO LIBRARY

Optical image of a whirlpool galaxy.

© JPL-CALTECH/STScI/VASSAR/NASA/SCIENCE PHOTO LIBRARY

Infrared composite image of colliding galaxies.

HST image of a planetary nebula – a series
of shells of gas cast off by a dying star.

© NASA/ESA/K. SAHU (STSCI/SWEEPS SCIENCE TEAM/SCIENCE PHOTO LIBRARY

A starfield where gravitational wobbles show significant extrasolar planets.

© NASA/ESA/G. BACON (STSCI)/SCIENCE PHOTO LIBRARY

Computer artwork of an extrasolar gas giant planet, orbiting a star in the constellation Vulpecula.

but she was still clinging to Homer. 'Close your eyes,' he shouted, 'and imagine Earth. I'll be right behind you, Annie. I'm coming with you. Try again – you can do this. Five! Four! Three! Two! *ONE!*'

Annie let go of Homer's leg and catapulted through the doorway. George flung himself after her, swinging around the doorframe and into another world – one he had never even dreamed of.

The doorway shut behind him as the dust cloud swallowed the whole of Mars, sweeping Homer's message and Annie and George's footprints off the surface and covering the little robot in a blanket of reddish dust. All that was left was the tiny red light on Homer's camera, winking away as he took photos of the Martian storm and sent them back to Annie's dad, so many millions of miles away on friendly planet Earth.

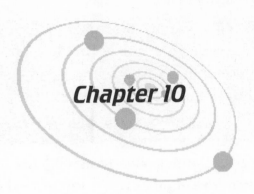

Chapter 10

Far away from the Global Space Agency headquarters, but really very close in terms of space distances, Daisy, George's mum, had just watched the sun rise over the Pacific Ocean. The sapphire night sky had changed to a light azure wash as the brilliant stars faded from view and the mist rose from the crystal-clear water. Daisy had been watching the sky all night.

As the Sun had set the day before, she had seen Mercury and Venus hang just over the horizon, disappearing as the Moon rose in the east. The night darkened and a million brilliant stars peppered the sky. Among them were Alpha and Beta Centauri, bright stars which both pointed the way to the Southern Cross, the great constellation that is only visible in the Southern Hemisphere. Daisy had lain back on the sands and looked into the heavens. Above her were the constellations Libra and Scorpius with the beautiful star and heart of Scorpius, Antares, shining down on her.

As she gazed at the stars, she thought of George at

the space-shuttle launch and imagined his excitement at seeing a real spacecraft lift off into the skies above. Little did she realize as she sat on the beach and looked upwards that George himself was somewhere out there in the Solar System, travelling between Mars and his next destination on the cosmic treasure hunt!

It was just as well that poor Daisy had no idea her son was, at that moment, lost in space – because George's dad, Terence, was currently lost on Earth – which was why she was sitting on the sand, waiting for the boat he'd taken to reappear. Terence and Daisy had gone to Tuvalu, a group of islands in the Pacific, a beautiful paradise lapped by a gentle blue sea. The sands were white, the palm trees waved and enormous butterflies and exotic birds fluttered amongst the thick vegetation.

But they hadn't gone there for a holiday. They had joined a group of their eco-warrior friends who were on a mission to chart the changes affecting these islands, islets and atolls.

The seas that looked so friendly, warm and inviting were actually rising, threatening to swallow up some of the tinier islands and leave no trace of life. Soon, all the people might lose their homes as the sea level got higher and higher. The ocean was rising because of a combination of melting land ice in the Antarctic, Greenland and the glaciers, coupled with the thermal expansion of sea water: as water warms up, it takes up more space,

which all adds up to more water and less land. Some of the islands and atolls were so low-lying that any change to the sea level became obvious very quickly as homes were flooded and beaches disappeared; the main runway in the capital city was now unusable for much of the year because it was often underwater.

The people could at least leave – even though they didn't want to lose their homes and their lives on those wonderful islands. But all the birds, butterflies and moths which had become used to that climate and that environment really didn't have anywhere else to go.

The Pacific Islanders had been trying to tell the rest of the world what was happening to them. They'd been to big conferences and made lots of noise about how their homes might not exist in a few years' time if global warming continued to make the sea rise at the same rate. Some people argued that the changes the Tuvaluans were experiencing were just part of a normal cycle of weather patterns that caused big storms to wash over the islands and drown them in monster tides. But others were convinced that what they saw

was a sign of something more sinister that couldn't be explained away so easily.

In a sense, the fact that Tuvalu seemed to be sinking was nothing new. The five atolls that made up the Tuvalu group had been sinking into the sea for a very long time. The famous explorer and naturalist Charles Darwin had sailed across the Pacific in 1835 and come up with an explanation for how atolls – which from above look like flat rings of sand surrounding a lagoon – had formed. New islands were created in tropical waters due to volcanic activity. Over millions of years, coral – organisms that live in warm shallow water – built up along the shoreline of these new volcanic islands as they sank back into the sea. Eventually the atoll would disappear altogether, but the coral would carry on growing up to the surface and above the water, forming reefs and beaches.

However, this process had taken place over a very long time – maybe as much as thirty million years. It was the past ten years and the next five that were giving the Tuvaluans serious cause for concern, and it was these rapid recent changes that they wanted to record.

In order to do this, George's dad, Terence, and a couple of others had left the main atoll by boat to explore the islands. But they hadn't come back when they were expected. They had taken maps for their journey but no GPS system or mobile phone. They had said they would navigate by the stars, just as another explorer, Captain Cook, had done all those years ago when he had sailed across the Southern Seas to record the transit of Venus across the Sun.

Unfortunately for Terence, they had got very lost and had not managed to find their way back to Tuvalu, where Daisy was now horribly worried about them. The other eco-activists had tried sending out boats to find them but they had come back with no sighting. Daisy and the others were growing frantic with worry – surely he and his friends didn't have enough fresh water on the boat to last long, and by day the sun

shines very brightly over the South Pacific. During that long night, Daisy had made a call to Florida to ask for help . . .

In another part of the Solar System, as George pushed himself through the doorway from Mars into the swirling dark orange world beyond, he heard Annie scream: 'It's all wet!'

George landed behind her on what looked like a sloping patch of frozen ground. He wobbled as he landed and reached back to grab hold of the doorframe to steady himself. Annie, who George had thrown through the doorway, seemed to fly slowly through the air, landing just next to a channel of dark liquid that flowed into an enormous black lake. For a second, it looked like she might topple over and fall into the black stream. But instead, she bent her knees, whirled her arms and took off, bounding gracefully over the dark river.

George hung onto the doorframe. The actual doorway back to Mars had closed b e h i n d him but the portal was still there, shimmering slightly in the dim light. He tested the ground with one space boot. It looked like it was made of solid ice. He tried to chip a bit off with his heel but it was as solid as granite. George looked around for something else to hold onto once the portal disappeared, but couldn't reach the rocks behind him and the slope in front was ice all the way down to the mysterious dark river.

'Whatever you do, don't fall in!' called Annie from the other side of the fast-moving liquid. 'We don't know what's in it!'

'Where are we?' called George, looking around. The skies above were very low and heavy, full of streaky orange and black clouds. The light was dim, as though it came from some far distant star across many millions of miles of space, and the clouds were so dense that the light struggled to reach the surface of this strange world. 'What is this place?'

'I don't know,' replied Annie. 'It feels like Earth before life began. You don't think Cosmos has sent us back in time by mistake, do you? Maybe he's transported us back to the beginning, to see what it was like before anything happened.'

The wind was apparently blowing very gently, but even so, it still packed a big punch as George tried to hang onto the portal doorway.

'George, this is ground control' – he heard Emmett's voice, sounding very serious – 'Cosmos can't hold the portal doorway in place for much longer. He needs to shut down that application, otherwise he might start malfunctioning.'

'Annie, what do I do?' asked George, who was suddenly terrified of tumbling into the stream and getting swept into the lake.

'You'll have to jump,' said Annie, 'like I did!' She was now standing on what looked like a tiny, icy beach on the other side of the channel, where it met the shore of the lake. 'It's flat here so you can land safely.' Beyond the little beach a craggy cliff face overhung the mysterious black lake, its peaks outlined against the glowing tiger-skin sky like a row of gigantic needles.

'There are too many applications open,' George heard Cosmos say. 'Portal will shut down instantly. If this has happened in error, please check the box to send a message to the support unit. Your feedback is important to us.'

The doorway vanished from view, leaving George and Annie by themselves on the mystery planet. Left with nothing to hold onto, George stumbled down the slope towards the black liquid. He pushed off from the ground, just as he had seen Annie do, which sent him upwards and across the stream . . .

'That wind is really strong!' he said, once he'd landed on the other side. All his movements felt as though they were happening in slow motion. 'It felt like it was trying to push me over! But it doesn't *seem* to be blowing very hard.'

'Maybe it's a thicker atmosphere than we have at home,' said Annie. 'Perhaps that's why it's like being in soup rather than being in air. And there's not much gravity here – that's why we're not falling very fast. Oh! What *is* that?' The clouds had just parted to allow them a view of this extraordinary world. On the other side of the lake they saw a huge mountain with a dip where the peak should have been.

'Wow! That looks like a dead volcano,' said George.

As they gazed at it, they saw the crater at the top

spew out great blobs of bluish liquid.

'I don't think it's dead!' shrieked Annie. The thick liquid was moving slowly down through the atmosphere to land on the slopes of the volcano, where it crept along like huge blind sticky earthworms, snaking down the side of the mountain.

'That looks disgusting!' she squeaked. 'What is it? And where are we? What planet are we on?'

'You're not on a planet,' Emmett radioed in finally. 'You're on Titan, the largest moon of Saturn. You are nearly one billion miles away, near to a cryovolcano, Ganesa Macula, which is currently erupting.'

'Is there any danger from the eruption?' asked George. They could see the strange thick lava creeping down channels carved into the rocky landscape.

'Bit hard to say,' replied Emmett cheerfully, 'given that no life form we know of has ever landed on Titan before.'

'Cheers, Emmett,' said George darkly.

'But the cryovolcanoes emit water – even though it is really cold water. It's mixed with ammonia, which means it can get down to minus one hundred degrees Celsius without freezing. So I shouldn't think it smells very nice. But that won't bother you, with your space-suits on.'

'Emmett, there are lakes here! And rivers!' said Annie. 'But they are weird and dark – it doesn't look like water.'

TITAN

Titan is the largest of Saturn's moons and the second largest moon in the Solar System. Only Ganymede – one of Jupiter's moons – is bigger.

Titan was discovered on 25 March 1655 by Dutch astronomer Christiaan Huygens. Huygens was inspired by Galileo's discovery of four moons around Jupiter. The discovery that Saturn had moons in orbit around it provided further proof for astronomers in the seventeenth century that not all objects in the Solar System travelled around the Earth, as was previously thought.

Saturn was thought to have seven moons but we now know there are at least 60 moons in orbit around the giant gas planet.

It takes 15 days and 22 hours for Titan to orbit Saturn – the same time as it takes for this moon to rotate once on its own axis, which means that a year on Titan is the same length as a day!

Titan is the only moon we know of in the Solar System that has a dense atmosphere. Before astronomers realized this, Titan itself was thought to be much larger in mass. Its atmosphere is mostly made up of nitrogen with a small amount of methane. Scientists think that it may be similar to the atmosphere of the early Earth and that Titan could have enough material to start the process of life. But this moon is very cold and lacks carbon dioxide so the chances of life existing there at the moment are slim.

Titan may show us what conditions on Earth were like in the very distant past and help us understand how life began here.

Titan is the most distant place on which a space probe has landed. On 1 July 2004 the Cassini-Huygens spacecraft reached Saturn. It flew by Titan on 26 October 2004 and the Huygens probe detached from the Cassini spacecraft and landed on Titan on 14 January 2005.

Huygens took photographs of Titan's surface and found that it rains there!

The probe also observed dry riverbeds – 'traces of once-flowing liquid' – on the surface. Cassini imaging later found evidence of hydrocarbons.

In billions of years' time, when our Sun becomes a red giant, Titan might become warm enough for life to begin!

© NASA/SCIENCE PHOTO LIBRARY

Artwork of the Cassini spacecraft approaching Saturn

'Why has Cosmos sent us here?' asked George.

'Once you and Annie had realized the clue led to one of the moons, Cosmos calculated that Titan was the most probable location for life of some kind to have existed, due to the chemical composition of its structure and atmosphere. Cosmos thinks you will find the next clue on Titan,' Emmett told them. 'Although I have to admit, he doesn't seem to know where. He's being a bit of a buzz-kill at the moment. Sometimes he's really helpful and then suddenly he starts sulking.'

'Oh, shut up! Stop hassling me,' complained Cosmos.

'Ooh, look!' said Annie, pointing towards the lake. 'What is it?' Drifting on the tide towards them, they saw a shape like a lifebuoy or a boat.

'It looks like a machine,' said George. 'Like something that came from Earth.'

'Unless,' said Annie, 'there's someone here and it belongs to them . . . Emmett,' she went on slowly, 'is there anyone out here? And if there is, do we want to meet them?'

'Um,' said Emmett, 'I'm trying to check on Cosmos, to see what he's got on his files for life on Titan.'

'No,' snapped Cosmos. 'I'm tired now. Don't wanna do any more work. Go 'way.'

'He's starting to run low on memory,' said Emmett. 'And we're going to need him to open up the portal to get you back fairly soon. So I'm looking in *The User's Guide* instead. Here we are – *Is There Anyone Out There?* This should tell us.'

IS THERE ANYONE OUT THERE?

Will some readers of this book walk on Mars? I hope so – indeed, I think it is very likely that they will. It will be a dangerous adventure and perhaps the most exciting exploration of all time. In earlier centuries, pioneer explorers discovered new continents, went to the jungles of Africa and South America, reached the North and South Poles and scaled the summits of the highest mountains. Those who travel to Mars will go in the same spirit of adventure.

It would be wonderful to traverse the mountains, canyons and craters of Mars, or perhaps even to fly over them in a balloon. But nobody would go to Mars for a comfortable life. It will be harder to live there than at the top of Everest or at the South Pole.

But the greatest hope of these pioneers would be to find something on Mars that was alive.

Here on Earth, there are literally millions of species of life – slime, moulds, mushrooms, trees, frogs, monkeys (and of course humans as well). Life survives in the most remote corners of our planet – in dark caves where sunlight has been blocked for thousands of years, on arid desert rocks, around hot springs where the water is at boiling point, deep underground and high in the atmosphere.

Our Earth teems with an extraordinary range of life forms. But there are constraints on size and shape. Big animals have fat legs but still can't jump like insects. The largest animals float in water. Far greater variety could exist on other planets. For instance, if gravity were weaker, animals could be larger and creatures our size could have legs as thin as insects'.

Everywhere you find life on Earth, you find *water*.

There is water on Mars and life of some kind could have emerged there. The red planet is much colder than the Earth and has a thinner atmosphere. Nobody expects green goggle-eyed Martians like those that feature in so many cartoons. If any advanced intelligent aliens existed on Mars, we would already know about them – and they might even have visited us by now!

Mercury and Venus are nearer the Sun than the Earth is. Both are very much hotter. Earth is the Goldilocks planet – not too hot and not too cold. If the Earth were too hot, even the most tenacious life would fry. Mars is a bit too cold but not absolutely frigid. The outer planets are colder still.

What about Jupiter, the biggest planet in our solar system? If life had evolved on this huge planet, where the force of gravity is far stronger than on Earth, it could be very strange indeed – for instance, huge balloon-like creatures, floating in the dense atmosphere.

Jupiter has four large moons which could, perhaps, harbour life. One of these, Europa, is covered in thick ice. Beneath that there lies an ocean. Perhaps there are creatures swimming in this ocean? To search for them, there are plans to send a robot in a submarine.

But the biggest moon in the Solar System is Titan, one of Saturn's many moons. Scientists have already landed a probe on Titan's surface, revealing rivers, lakes and rocks. But the temperature is about minus 170 degrees Celsius, where any water is frozen solid. It is not water but liquid methane that flows in these rivers and lakes – not a good place for life.

Let's now widen our gaze beyond our solar system to other stars. There are tens of billions of these suns in our galaxy. Even the nearest of these is so far away that, at the speed of a present-day rocket, it would take millions of years to reach it. Equally, if clever aliens existed on a planet orbiting another star, it would be difficult for them to visit us. It would be far easier to send a radio or laser signal than to traverse the mind-boggling distances of interstellar space.

If there was a signal back, it might come from aliens very different from us. Indeed, it could come from machines whose creators have long ago been usurped or become extinct. And, of course, there may be aliens who exist and have big 'brains' but are so different from us that we wouldn't recognize them or be able to communicate with them. Some may not want to reveal that they exist (even if they are actually watching us!). There may be some super-intelligent dolphins, happily thinking profound thoughts deep under some alien ocean, doing nothing to reveal their presence. Still other 'brains' could actually be swarms of insects, acting together like a single intelligent being. There may be a lot more out there than we could ever detect. Absence of evidence isn't evidence of absence.

There are billions of planets in our galaxy and our galaxy itself is only one of billions. Most people would guess that the cosmos is teeming with life – but that would be no more than a guess. We still know too little about how life began, and how it evolves, to be able to say whether simple life is common. We know even less about how likely it would be for simple life to evolve in the way it did here on Earth. My bet (for what it is worth) is that simple life is indeed very common but that intelligent life is much rarer.

Indeed, there may not be any intelligent life out there at all. Earth's intricate biosphere could be unique. Perhaps we really are alone. If that's true, it's a disappointment for those who are looking for alien signals – or who even hope that some day aliens may visit us. But the failure of searches needn't depress us. Indeed, it is perhaps a reason to be cheerful because we can then be less modest about our place in the great scheme of things. Our Earth could be the most interesting place in the cosmos.

If life *is* unique to the Earth, it could be seen as just a cosmic sideshow – though it needn't be. That is because evolution isn't over – indeed, it could be nearer its beginning that its end. Our Solar System is barely middle-aged – it will be 6 billion years before the Sun swells up, engulfs the inner planets and vaporizes any life that still remains on Earth. Far-future life and intelligence could be as different from us as we are from a bug. Life could spread from Earth through the entire Galaxy, evolving into a teeming complexity far beyond what we can even imagine. If so, our tiny planet – this pale-blue dot floating in space – could be the most important place in the entire cosmos.

Martin

'Is there anyone out there?' said Emmett. 'I think probably not – at least, not where you are. So far, I think it's just you and the lakes of methane.'

'Ugh! It's raining!' said Annie. She held out one hand to catch a raindrop. Huge drops of liquid, three times the size of raindrops on Earth, were falling from the sky. But they didn't fall fast and straight, like normal rain. They dawdled in the atmosphere, wafting and twirling around like snowflakes.

'Oh no!' said Emmett. 'It must be methane rain! I don't know how much pure methane your spacesuits can withstand before they start to deteriorate.'

'Hang on a minute . . .' George peered at the strange boat which was drifting towards the shoreline.

'Huh!' said Annie, rather sharply. 'I am just hanging about. There isn't much else to do round here.'

'It's got some writing on it!' said George.

'Ooh, spooky!' Annie leaned forward to get a better look as the huge raindrops sploshed gently on her space helmet. 'It does too. I can see it now . . . Well, bonanza!' she said, staring at the round object, which was now marooned on the shore of the lake. 'Look at that! It did come from Earth! It's got human writing on it!'

In big letters on the side of the frozen object they saw the words: HUYGENS.

'Emmett, it says "Huygens" on it,' Annie reported. 'What does that mean? It isn't a bomb, is it?'

'No way!' replied Emmett. 'It means you've found

the Huygens probe – the one they sent to Titan! I don't think it works any more but that's still pretty cool. Literally cool. Like minus one hundred and seventy degrees Celsius cool!'

'But that's not all!' Annie exclaimed. 'It's got some other writing on it too! It's got alien letters on it!'

On the other side of her, George now had a clear view. 'It's a message in a bottle!' he cried. 'Except it isn't! It's a message on a probe.'

Painted onto the probe was another row of pictures . . .

Chapter 11

Back on Earth, Emmett was sitting on the floor in the middle of the Clean Room, with both Cosmos and *The User's Guide to the Universe* open in front of him, when he heard a commotion. The cleaning machines at the entry point suddenly whirred into life and a flashing red sign above the door lit up. DECONTAMINATING, it said, beeping loudly as it flashed. Emmett hadn't noticed the sign on his way in because he was too busy being brushed, buffed and popped into his white suit by the machine. But he was hardly going to ignore it now. It meant that someone was coming in!

He leaped to his feet, his heart pounding. He didn't want to move Cosmos, who was ready to transfer Annie and George from Titan to wherever they thought they might find the next clue. But neither did he want Cosmos to be interrupted by someone who might mess around with him while he was performing such an important and difficult operation.

Emmett suddenly spotted what looked like a length

of shiny yellow cooking foil. In fact, it was the covering used to protect probes from overheating in the Sun's rays as they travelled through space. He gently arranged it around Cosmos and then stood in front of the computer, trying to strike a carefree and nonchalant pose, as though he always wandered into Clean Rooms and lurked around large machinery being prepared for space travel. He readjusted his face mask in the hope that whoever came in might not realize that he was, in fact, a kid and would just assume he was a very small Clean Room operative.

A figure was ejected into the Clean Room from the decontamination machine. It staggered a bit, weaving around in its white suit until it had found its feet. It was impossible to guess who it might be – even more so because the decontamination machine seemed to have put the head covering and face mask on backwards, so where there should have been eyes and a chin there was just dark hair.

'Youch!' the figure cried, tripping over a half-assembled satellite. 'Oh, colliding hadrons!' It hopped from foot to foot. 'I've stubbed my toe! Ouch! Ouch!'

Emmett got a sick feeling in his stomach. It felt like it did when he ate some foods that he knew he was allergic to. There was only one person it could be underneath the white suit and he was about the last person Emmett wanted to see right now.

The hopping figure stopped dancing around and ripped off his back-to-front face mask and head gear. It was, of course, Eric.

'Ahh,' he said, looking down at Emmett, disguised in his white suit. 'Do you, by any chance, work here?'

'Er, yes, yes, I do!' said Emmett in his deepest voice. 'Absolutely. Have done so for years. Many many many many many many years. I'm really ancient, in fact. You just can't tell because I've got my face mask on.'

'It's just that you look, a bit . . . well, a touch, perhaps . . .'

'I was taller,' said Emmett in his grown-up voice. 'But I got so old I shrank.'

'Yes, yes, interesting,' said Eric calmly. 'Well, the thing is, Mr . . .'

'Hm, hm . . .' Emmett cleared his throat. 'Professor, if you don't mind.'

'Of course, Professor . . . ?'

Emmett panicked. 'Professor Spock,' he said wildly.

'Professor . . . Spock,' repeated Eric slowly.

'Er, yes,' said Emmett. 'That's right. Professor Spock from the University of . . . Enterprise.'

'Well, Professor Spock,' said Eric, 'I wonder if you

could help me. I'm looking for some kids who I seem to have lost. And maybe you've seen them somewhere around here? Or, being so wise and so very old, you might have an idea where they've got to? They were seen coming this way by a security camera.'

'Kids?' repeated Emmett gruffly. 'Can't stand them. Don't have any of them in my Clean Room. No, not never. Not kids.'

'The thing is,' said Eric gently, 'I really do need to find them. For a start, I'm worried about them and I'd like to know that they're OK. But also because we've got an emergency situation going on and it involves one of the missing kids.'

'It does?' said Emmett, forgetting to use his adult voice.

'Actually it's about his father,' Eric told him.

'His father?' Emmett whipped off his face mask. 'Is my dad OK? Has anything happened to him?' Tears filled his eyes.

'No, Emmett,' said Eric, putting an arm around him and patting him on the back. 'It isn't your dad. It's George's.'

Eric started to tell Emmett the story of George's dad – where he'd gone and why, and how he'd got lost in the South Pacific – but he was interrupted by the sound of the decontamination machine starting up again. '*Beep! Beep!*' The red light over the door flashed as yet another person entered the machine.

'Get your nasty robot hands off me!' They heard an outraged shout. 'I'm an old lady! Show some respect!'

There was a crunching noise and the machinery seemed to grind to a halt, followed by a stamping of feet as the door was pushed open and a very cross-looking old lady clutching a walking cane and a handbag – both neatly wrapped in white plastic – burst through.

The beeping noise had stopped and the red light was frozen in mid-flash.

'What in heaven's name was all that about?' demanded the old lady. She wasn't wearing a white outfit at all – just her usual tweed suit. 'I will not be treated like that by some blasted machine. Ah, Eric!' she said as she spotted him.

'I've found you. You can't get away from me, you know.'

'I'm starting to realize that,' murmured Eric.

'What was that? I'm deaf – you'll have to write it down.' She ripped off the plastic covering from her handbag and rummaged around for her notebook.

'Emmett,' said Eric in resigned tones, 'this is Mabel, George's grandmother. She arrived here today to ask for my help in locating George's dad, Terence – who, as I told you, is lost in the South Pacific. The emergency alert I received earlier – it turned out to be from Mabel, who George's mum, Daisy, had contacted.' He took Mabel's notebook and scribbled: *Mabel, this is Emmett. He is George's friend and he is just about to tell me where George and Annie have got to.*

Mabel looked over at Emmett and smiled, a real smile full of friendliness and warmth. 'Oh, Eric!' she said. 'What a terrible memory you have! Emmett and I met at the airport so we are old friends already. Remember though, I'm very deaf, so if you want to talk to me you'll have to write it down.'

'Live long and prosper,' said Emmett, giving her the Vulcan salute with one hand and writing his greeting in her book with the other.

'Thank you, Emmett,' replied Mabel. 'I have indeed lived a very long time and prospered greatly.' She saluted him back again.

'But I don't understand. How are you going to

rescue George's dad if he's in the Pacific and you're here?' Emmett asked Eric. 'Are you going to send a rocket to pick him up?'

'Ah, well, you forget,' said Eric. 'I – well, the Global Space Agency actually – have satellites which orbit the Earth. Space missions don't just look outward across the cosmos, they also look back at Earth so we can see what's happening on our own planet. So I've asked the satellite department to look closely at that part of the Pacific Ocean and see if they can spot Terence. Once we know where he is, we can let Daisy and his friends know and they can send someone out to rescue him. So fingers crossed, Terence is going to be OK.'

SATELLITES IN SPACE

A satellite is an object that orbits – or revolves – around another object, like the Moon around the Earth. The Earth is a satellite of the Sun. However, we tend to use the word 'satellite' to mean the man-made objects that are sent into space on a rocket to perform certain tasks, such as navigation, weather monitoring or communication.

Rockets were invented by the ancient Chinese in around 1000 AD. Many hundreds of years later, on 4 October 1957, the Space Age began for real when the Russians used a rocket to launch the first satellite into orbit around the Earth. Sputnik, a small sphere capable of sending a weak radio signal back to Earth, became a sensation. At the time, it was known as the 'Red Moon' and people all over the world tuned their radios to pick up its signal. The Mark I telescope at Jodrell Bank in the UK was the first large radio telescope to be used as a tracking antenna to chart the course of the satellite. Sputnik was quickly followed by Sputnik II – also called 'Pupnik' because it had a passenger on board! Laika, a Russian dog, became the first living being from Earth to travel into space.

The Americans tried to launch their own satellite on 6 December 1957 but the satellite only managed to get 1.2 metres off the ground before the rocket exploded. On 1 February 1958 Explorer I was more successful, and soon the two superpowers on Earth – the USSR and the USA – were also competing to be the greatest in space. At that time, they were very suspicious of each other and soon realized that satellites were good for spying. Using photographs taken from above the Earth, the two superpowers hoped to learn more about activities in the other country. The satellite revolution had begun.

Satellite technology was originally developed for military and intelligence reasons. In the 1970s the US government launched 24 satellites, which sent back time signals and orbital information. This led to the first global positioning system (GPS). This technology, which allows armies to cross deserts by night and long-range missiles to hit targets accurately, is now used by millions of ordinary car drivers to avoid getting lost! Known as satellite navigation – or sat nav – it also helps ambulances to reach the injured more promptly and coastguards to launch effective search and rescue missions.

SATELLITES IN SPACE cont . . .

Communication across the world was also changed for ever by satellites. In 1962 a US telephone company launched Telstar, a satellite that broadcast the first ever live television show from the US to Britain and France. The British saw only a few minutes of fuzzy pictures but the French received clear pictures and sound. They even managed to send back their own transmission of Yves Montand singing 'Relax, You Are in Paris'! Before satellites, events had to be filmed and the film taken by plane to be shown on television in other countries. After Telstar, major world events – such as the funeral of US President John F. Kennedy in 1963, or the World Cup in 1966 – could be broadcast live across the globe for the first time. Mobile phones and the internet are other ways in which you might be using a satellite today.

Satellite imaging isn't used only by spies! Being able to look back at the Earth from space has enabled us to see patterns, both on the Earth and in the atmosphere. We can measure land use and see how cities are expanding and how deserts and forests are changing shape. Farmers use satellite pictures to monitor their crops and decide which fields need fertilizer.

And satellites have transformed our understanding of the weather. They have made weather forecasts more accurate and shown the way weather patterns emerge and move around the world. Satellites cannot change the weather but they can track hurricanes, tornadoes and cyclones, giving us the ability to issue severe weather warnings.

In the late 1990s NASA's TOPEX/Poseidon satellite, which maps the oceans, provided enough information for weather watchers to spot the El Niño phenomenon. And Jason, a new series of NASA satellites, has recently been launched to gather data about the ocean's role in determining the Earth's climate. This in turn will help us to understand climate change better, showing us detailed images of the melting polar ice caps, disappearing inland seas and rising ocean levels – information we now need urgently!

Earthrise over Moon, taken by US astronauts on board Apollo 8, 1968.

It is one of the first images of the Earth seen from another world.

Mars

Mars close approach, taken by the Hubble Space Telescope, 2007.

Martian erosion features.

Phoenix lander image
of ice on Mars.

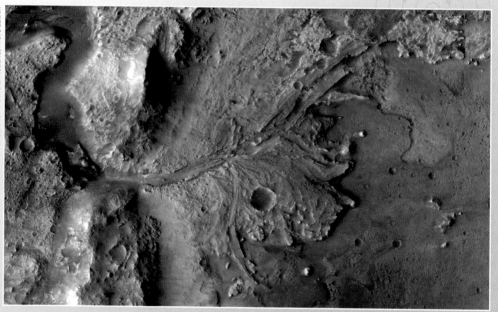

Colour-enhanced satellite image of a Martian river delta.

Titan

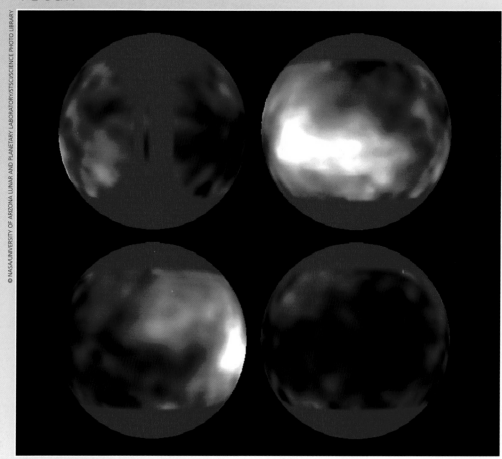

HST image of Titan's surface, 1994. Top left is hemisphere facing Saturn, bottom right is hemisphere facing away from Saturn.

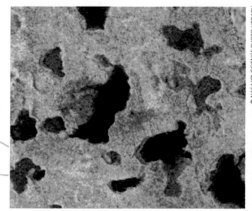

Cassini image of hydrocarbon lakes on Titan.

Cassini image of surface features on Titan.

HST image of Titan orbiting Saturn, 1995.

ALPHA CENTAURI

X-ray image of Alpha Centauri, showing the two brightest stars in the system.

55 CANCRI

Artwork of the planets and their orbits in the 55 Cancri binary star system.

Artwork of extrasolar planet around 55 Cancri.

EARTH

Earth from space, in true colour,
showing Europe and northern Africa.

Just as satellites can look back at the Earth and transform our understanding of our own planet, so they have also changed our perception of the Universe around us. The Hubble Space Telescope was the first large-scale space observatory. Orbiting the Earth, Hubble has helped astronomers to calculate the age of the Universe and has shown that it is expanding at an accelerated pace.

There are 3,000 satellites in orbit around the Earth, with a total coverage of every square centimetre of the planet. It is getting quite crowded out there and can be dangerous. Satellites in low Earth orbit move very fast – around 18,000 miles an hour. Collisions are rare but when they happen, they make a mess! Even a fleck of paint moving at that speed could cause damage if it hit a spacecraft. There may be a million pieces of space junk orbiting the Earth, but only about 9,000 of these are bigger than a tennis ball.

'Couldn't the satellites also measure the rising sea?' asked Emmett.

'Well, yes, they could,' said Eric. 'And I would have happily helped them, if only they'd asked me. But even so, human exploration and real experience are still very important. On their journey they will have learned a lot about other things that satellites can't help us with. But we could have worked together on this project. And perhaps we will now. Daisy called Mabel to tell her that Terence was missing and Mabel came straight here to find me. Which was, of course, exactly the right thing to do. Any minute now, we should spot him,' he finished, just a touch smugly. 'Anyway, where are George and Annie? Have you been playing hide-and-seek?' He smiled and Emmett's heart leaped into his mouth.

'We are playing a sort of game,' he stuttered.

'Oh good!' said Eric. 'MABEL, THE KIDS ARE PLAYING A GAME! Tell us – we can all join in. I could do with some fun, what with having missed the launch.'

'Y'know, like, a treasure hunt,' said Emmett slowly.

'Ye-esss . . .' said Eric.

'A game?' asked Mabel. 'How exciting!'

'Like, where you have clues and you have to follow them to find out where you need to go,' continued Emmett, wishing he could blast himself into space at that exact moment and not have to finish what he had to say.

Eric scribbled something in Mabel's notebook.

'A treasure hunt! How splendid!' she exclaimed, reading it. 'My, it's not just your memory, Eric! Your handwriting is dreadful too. How ever did you get so far in life?'

'So what's the clue? Where have they gone?'

Eric was still smiling when Cosmos, from under his reflective thermal blanket, said in a loud voice, *'Ping! Sending is complete! Mission stage three is underway.'* Eric stopped smiling as soon as he heard Cosmos's voice. He ran over to the shiny pile of crumpled foil and whisked it away to reveal the super-computer underneath. 'THAT'S MY COMPUTER!' he shouted so loudly that even Mabel heard him with no problem. 'So where in the Universe are Annie and George?'

Chapter 12

Eric looked so angry that, for one horrifying moment, Emmett had a flash vision of him exploding like a supernova in a burst of radiation that was so bright it could outshine a whole galaxy. He glared at Emmett, the full force of nuclear fury blazing in his eyes.

'If you've done what I think you've done . . .' he said.

Emmett just opened and closed his mouth like a goldfish. He tried to speak but he couldn't get any sound out. He made a strange sort of gurgling noise instead.

'Where are Annie and George?' asked Eric quietly but fiercely, his face white with tension.

'A . . . a . . . a . . .' was all Emmett could stutter.

Mabel's bright eyes were flicking from Eric to Emmett as she tried to work out what was going on.

'Tell me,' said Eric. 'I need to know.'

Emmett moved his lips but he still couldn't make his voice work. He swallowed loudly as tears filled his eyes.

'Right!' said Eric. 'If you refuse to tell me, then I'll ask Cosmos instead.' He knelt down on the floor in front of the computer and started tapping away furiously. 'How could you!' he muttered to himself. 'How could you do this!'

Mabel hobbled over to Emmett and handed him her notepad and pencil.

'If there's something that's too difficult to say,' she whispered to him, 'perhaps you could write it down instead? Then anything you need to tell Eric, I can say for you.'

Emmett looked at her gratefully and took them. He chewed the pencil end, not sure where to start.

'What if I ask you some questions?' said Mabel kindly. 'That might get us going. Why is Eric so upset?'

He's mad because we took his special computer, Cosmos, Emmett wrote neatly in Mabel's book.

'What's so special about Cosmos?' asked Mabel.

He can send you across the Universe.

'Have Annie and George gone on a trip?'

Emmett nodded, his big eyes full of fear. But Mabel just smiled at him and motioned for him to carry on writing. He took a big gulp and put pen to paper again. *They were on Titan but they've just gone through the portal to the nearest star system to us, Alpha Centauri. They think this is where they will find the next clue. The first clue came to them on Earth, they got the second on Mars and the third on Titan.*

'Ah, the treasure hunt.' Mabel nodded understandingly.

Eric was still bashing away on Cosmos, who didn't seem to be helping him. 'Bog off! Access denied!' said the super-computer angrily. Emmett glanced nervously at them.

'Who is leaving these clues for them?' said Mabel.

We don't know, wrote Emmett. *But each message has the same ending – it threatens to destroy planet Earth if we don't follow them.*

'Any more clues about the clues?'

Well, wrote Emmett, doodling a little. *I did work*

something out. But I might be wrong . . . He drew a series of dots.

'Carry on,' said Mabel as Eric let out a howl of frustration. She put a calming hand on Emmett's shoulder. 'We'll deal with him in a minute.'

The first clue came to them on Earth, where there is already life. The second clue was on Mars, where we think there might have been life in the past. The third clue was on Titan, which is a moon of Saturn. Titan might be like the Earth was just before life began. So we thought the fourth clue might take them to Alpha

Centauri, which is the nearest star system to us and the closest place we would look for signs of life outside the Solar System. And they have to find a planet in a binary star system. That's what the clue says.

'So you think they are following a trail of life in the Universe in order to prevent life on Earth from coming to an end,' said Mabel. 'You are a very smart boy, Emmett. Eric!' She poked him in the back with her cane.

'Leave. Me. Alone. I. Am. Busy,' said Eric as Cosmos blew a loud raspberry at him.

'Well, hard cheese to you!' said Mabel. 'I've got something to say. And when you get to my age, you have the right to speak, whether anyone wants you to or not. Eric, you have scared this poor boy so much he can't tell you what he knows. So if you could try and be a bit nicer to him, he will stop feeling so terrified and help you sort this out.'

That boy, wrote Eric in Mabel's book, *has put Annie and George in terrible danger. I am incandescent.*

'We can see that,' said Mabel. 'But you are also wasting valuable time and you need to listen. And stop blaming Emmett.'

Eric really did explode this time. 'Somehow he managed to repair my computer without telling me,' he ranted. 'And then he let Annie and George go off across the Universe, chasing after some crank message Annie imagined she'd received through a computer, which at the time didn't even work, from aliens who don't exist. And now Cosmos is malfunctioning again and we have no idea if we can ever get them back!'

Mabel had clearly heard every word. 'Oh, stop it!' she snapped. 'This isn't Emmett's fault. This is entirely the work of your daughter and my grandson. It's got their sticky fingerprints all over it. George told me he had to come to Florida because Annie had something important she wanted him to do. And this must be it. They have gone on a mission because they believe the Earth is in danger and they need to do something about it. They received the first clue on Earth, but Emmett here tells me that when they followed it to Mars, they found another clue waiting for them. That clue sent them to Titan. They've just left Titan and gone to look for a planet around' – Mabel checked her notebook – 'Alpha Centauri.'

'What?' said Eric. 'You mean they haven't gone out there just for fun, for messing around? You mean they've actually gone to one location, found a clue and then gone *further* out?'

Emmett nodded, his eyes squeezed tight shut.

'How in the name of Einstein could that happen?' asked Eric in disbelief.

'Um, I created a remote portal application when I was updating Cosmos,' whispered Emmett, finding a bit of his voice again. 'I'm really sorry.'

Eric took his glasses off and rubbed his eyes. 'And you say they got to Mars and found another clue waiting for them?'

'Yup,' said Emmett. 'It was drawn on the surface of Mars by Homer's tyres.'

Eric put his glasses back on and sprang to his feet. 'Emmett' – he took the boy by his shoulders – 'I'm sorry I shouted at you. I really am. But I need to reach Annie and George immediately. Can you send me out to Alpha Centauri?'

Emmett sagged a little. 'I can try,' he said nervously. 'But Cosmos is being a bit difficult and I'm worried that he is using too much memory now. I don't know what will happen if I send another person through the portal.'

But Eric had already gone to get his spacesuit.

Emmett plonked himself down cross-legged in front of Cosmos. Mabel stood over him. 'My poor old joints won't let me get down that far,' she said regretfully.

'Oh!' said Emmett. Immediately he got to his feet, picked up Cosmos and balanced him on the side of the half-assembled satellite so that George's gran could see the screen. He fetched some spare machinery parts, which he arranged as a sort of chair so that Mabel could sit down.

'Thank you, Emmett,' she said. 'That's very considerate of you.'

'My pleasure,' he said seriously. He tried to arrange some of the shiny yellow foil as a blanket over Mabel's knees but she batted him away.

'Go on with you!' she said affectionately. 'Get to your computer and don't worry about this old dear.'

Nervously Emmett entered his personal password, waiting to see if Cosmos would react as badly to him as he had done to Eric. 'Access granted,' said Cosmos politely. Emmett then typed in a command for locating

the last portal activity so that he could create another doorway from Earth and send Eric through it to where Annie and George had gone. But this time it wasn't Cosmos's attitude that worried Emmett so much. It was his ability to perform the tasks they so badly needed him to do.

'Planet . . . orbit . . . Alpha Centauri . . .' said Cosmos slowly. 'Seeking co-ordinates for last portal activity in the Alpha Centauri star system . . . seeking . . . planet in orbit . . . seeking information . . . seeking last portal location . . .' The little hourglass appeared on Cosmos's screen. Emmett pressed a few keys but Cosmos did not respond. All that happened was that the little hourglass flashed a few times, as though to remind Emmett that Cosmos was busy.

I think he is running out of memory, Emmett wrote in Mabel's notebook as they waited. *He's using so much of it at the moment to operate these portals in distant space. It's really important we don't ask him too many difficult questions right now.*

'What do we need to know?' asked Mabel.

We need to know where Cosmos sent Annie and George. They asked him to find them a planet in the Alpha Centauri star system.

'And how do you find a planet in space . . . ?'

HOW TO FIND A PLANET IN SPACE

Planets don't generate their own energy, leaving them very dim compared to their nuclear-powered home stars. If you use a powerful telescope to take a picture of a planet, its faint light will be lost in the glare of the star it orbits.

However, planets can be detected by the gravitational pull they exert on their star. Planets pull apples, moons and satellites towards them by gravity, and they also pull on their home star. Just as a dog on a leash can yank its owner around, a planet can pull its home star around, with the leash being gravity.

Astronomers can watch a nearby star, especially a close one such as Alpha Centauri A or B, to see if it is being yanked around by an unseen planet. The responsive motion of a star is a telltale sign of a planet, and that motion can be detected in two ways.

Firstly, the light waves from the star are either compressed or stretched as it approaches or recedes from us on Earth (this is called the Doppler Effect).

Secondly, two telescopes acting as one can combine the light waves from a star to detect the motion of that star.

Planets as small as Earth and as large as Jupiter can be detected using these techniques.

Maybe one day *you* will find a planet that no one has ever spotted before!

Geoff

Chapter 13

'Eeew!' said Annie, shielding her eyes with her arm as they stepped through the portal from Titan onto the planet Cosmos had found for them in orbit around the star Alpha Centauri B. Fortunately, after a few seconds, the special glass in her space helmet visor darkened and her vision started coming back.

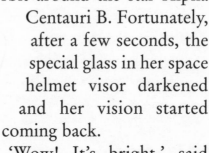

'Wow! It's bright,' said George, stepping through after her. This time they thought they were better prepared than when they had landed on Mars and Titan. They had got out the emergency rope and the metal pegs that came with their spacesuits, ready to tether themselves to the surface of their new planet. But when they stepped through the doorway, they found that for once they didn't float off. Instead, they felt much heavier than they did on Earth.

They could still walk, but it was an effort to pick up each leg to move forward.

'Oof!' said Annie, dropping the rope and the pegs. 'I'm feel like I'm being squished.' It was as though someone was pushing her towards the bleached ground.

'More gravity!' said George. 'We must be on a planet similar to Earth but with a greater mass so we feel the gravity more strongly than we would do at home. But it can't be that much greater or we'd crushed by now.'

'I'm going to sit down,' puffed Annie. 'I'm really tired.'

'No! Don't!' said George. 'You might never get up again. You mustn't sit down, Annie, or we'll never get away from here.'

Annie groaned and leaned on him. She felt like a ton weight and George staggered to stay upright and hold onto her at the same time.

'Annie, we've got to find the next clue and leave,' he said urgently. 'There's too much gravity here for us – we weren't built to exist in conditions like these. If we were ants, we'd be OK. But we're too big for high-gravity places. And it's too shiny. My eyes are starting to hurt.'

Where Mars – and certainly Titan – had been much darker than the Earth, this new planet was blindingly bright. Even with the dark space visors protecting their eyes like super-strength sunglasses, it was still difficult to see. 'Don't look directly at the sun,' warned George.

'It's even brighter than our Sun at home.'

Not that there was much to look at. Around them stretched miles of bald rock, baking in the brilliant light beaming down on this heavy, hot planet. George gazed around anxiously, looking for some sign that would lead them to the fourth clue.

'Whass . . . that . . . over . . . there?' Annie, who was now leaning on him entirely, flapped an arm in one direction. Her speech had become very slow and slurred.

George shook her. 'Annie! Wake up! Wake up!' The light and the weight of this weird planet seemed to be drugging her. He tried to call Cosmos or Emmett. The first time, he got an engaged tone, the second a recorded message saying: *'Your call is important to us. Press hash key plus one to be put through to—'* But then he was cut off.

Annie flopped onto him. She was so heavy on this planet – it was like trying to carry a baby elephant. George stood there, Annie's head on his shoulder

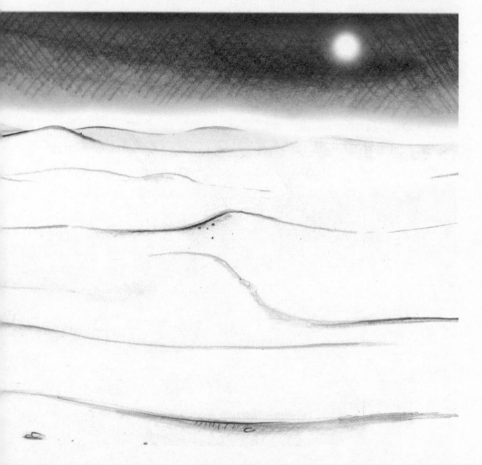

and his arms around her. He started to feel really scared. He imagined that in years to come, when the first interstellar travellers made the journey to this unnamed planet in orbit around one of the nearest stars to Earth, they might find the scorched remains of two human children, frazzled and boiled into fragments on the parched surface. Somewhat dazed himself, he pictured them leaping off their spaceship to claim this new planet, only to find that two kids had once made the four light-year journey to this infernal place in order to perish under its burning star.

But just as he was giving up hope and starting to sag towards the ground, the light in the sky began to dim a little. It was changing from brilliant white to a softer yellow.

'Look, Annie!' he said, shaking her in his arms. 'The sun's going down! You're going to be OK! Just hold on for a few minutes more. It's moving across the

sky pretty quickly – well, quicker than the Sun back home on Earth, anyway. Once it goes down, we'll be able to cool off and find the clue.'

'Huh?' said Annie blearily. She raised her head from his shoulder and stared out behind him. 'But it's not going down! It's coming up . . . it's really pretty,' she went on dreamily. 'Bright shiny star rising in the sky . . .'

'Annie, it's not going up!' said George, who thought she must be hallucinating. 'Concentrate! The sun is going down, not up!' The light around them was dimming gently.

'Don't be silly!' Annie sounded annoyed, her voice slightly stronger. George felt relieved – if she could get cross with him, then she was definitely feeling better. 'I know up from down, and I tell you it's going up!'

They moved apart by a few centimetres and stood staring over each other's shoulders.

'It's that way,' said Annie, pointing.
'Up!'

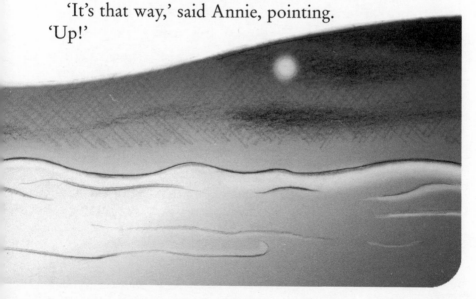

'No, it's over there!' said George. 'Down!'

'Turn round,' ordered Annie.

George turned round very slowly – it wasn't possible to move fast on the high-gravity planet – and saw she was right. There was a small bright sun in the sky behind him, rising over the rocky planet. It didn't give the same glaring light as the sun setting on the other side of the planet, but it shone a gentle beam on them, meaning that it would not often be dark on this bright, barren planet.

'Of course! We're in a binary star system, just like it showed us in the clue! This planet has two suns!' said George. 'I'm sure I've read about this system on the net. One sun is bigger than the other – that one setting must be Alpha B, the star this planet orbits. It looks bigger because we're closer to it. And the other one must be Alpha A, the other star in the Centauri system. Alpha A is actually larger, but we're further away from it.'

Now that the light was growing softer, they could make out more of the landscape around them. Quite nearby they saw the lip of a huge hole in the ground.

'Let's go and have a look in there,' said Annie.

'Because . . . ?' questioned George.

'There isn't anywhere else to look!' She shrugged. 'And maybe there's another clue down there. On both Mars and Titan, Cosmos sent us really close to each new clue. Have you got any better suggestions?' She seemed quite restored to her usual difficult self.

'Nope,' said George. He tried calling Emmett again but just got the engaged tone once more.

'Come on,' said Annie, 'but I'm not walking.' She dropped to her hands and knees and started to crawl towards the crater.

George tried to walk, but it was so difficult and slow – he felt like the Tin Man in *The Wizard of Oz*, having to throw each leg forward in order to move. So he too got down on his hands and knees and followed Annie, who was now peering over the edge to see what lay at the bottom.

'There's nothing there,' she said in disappointment, looking into the gaping empty crater formed by a collision with a comet or an asteroid.

George wriggled up beside her. 'Then where will we find the next cl—?' he started to say. But he stopped. Because just then, at the very bottom of the huge crater, they saw something they definitely weren't expecting. Faintly, but getting more solid by the second, they saw the outline of a doorway. And at the same moment as one space boot and then another stepped through it, the transmission device in George's helmet buzzed into life.

'George!' he heard. 'This is your grandmother speaking!'

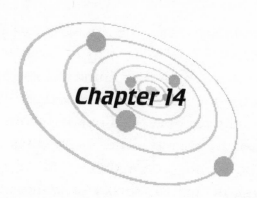

Chapter 14

At the bottom of the crater, Eric stepped smartly through the portal and promptly fell flat on his face. He had prepared his telling-off speech to the kids while he was getting ready to walk through Cosmos's doorway. But once he reached the distant planet, all he came out with was 'Nrrgghh!'

'Dad!' cried Annie from the top of the crater, and burst into tears inside her space helmet. She no longer cared whether he was going to be cross with her. She just felt overjoyed to see him. She slithered over the crater's lip and wriggled down towards him on her tummy. As Eric rolled over onto his back, Annie crashed into him and gave him a great big hug.

'Dad!' she sobbed. 'It's so nasty here! I don't like this planet.'

Eric gave a huge sigh that Emmett and Mabel heard many millions of miles away on planet Earth, and decided to save his speech about kids who travelled through space by themselves when they shouldn't for another time. He hugged Annie instead.

George's gran had no such reservations. 'George!' she said sternly over the link from Earth. 'I can't believe you roped me into this dangerous scheme without telling me! I'm very angry that you didn't see fit to properly inform me why you wanted to come to America . . .' She banged on and on, and George wished he could turn down the volume, as Emmett had done with Cosmos. But then he looked into the crater and saw Eric beckoning George to come and join them.

'Sorry, Gran!' said George. 'I have to go! We'll talk later.' And he slid down the side of the enormous hole to join Eric and Annie, ending up in a group hug in spacesuits at the bottom of the crater on an unnamed planet orbiting Alpha B in the Alpha Centauri star system.

'I've got to close down the portal for a few minutes,' came Emmett's voice. 'I can't hold the portal and do all the other things I need to with Cosmos. So don't panic when the doorway vanishes. I'll get it straight back to you.'

The portal doorway became translucent and started to fade away. George, Annie and Eric lay back against the curved surface of the crater's wall and gazed at Alpha A, moving across the clear, dark blue sky.

'So, George and Annie,' said Eric as they lay on either side of him, 'here we all are, together, once again. Lost in space, once again.' By now, the portal had completely disappeared.

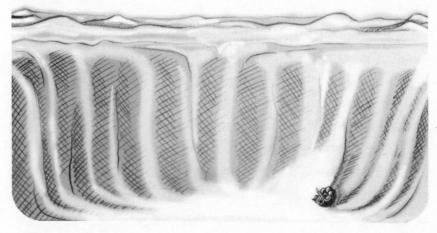

'Can we go home now?' sniffed Annie. 'I've had enough of this.'

'Soon, very soon,' said Eric calmly. 'Just as soon as Emmett gets the reverse portal working again.'

'What!' exclaimed George, trying to sit up but finding he didn't have the strength left to fight gravity. He lay back down again. 'You mean we can't go back to Earth?'

'I'm afraid not,' said Eric quietly. 'Cosmos is having some problems, but Emmett will sort them out. I wouldn't have left him in charge if I weren't sure he was the best person for the job. He's already done things with Cosmos I couldn't even dream of.'

'You mean you came here to find us even though you knew we might not be able to get back?' said Annie. 'That we might be stuck here for ever?'

'Of course I did,' said Eric. 'I couldn't leave you out here by yourselves, could I?'

'Oh, Dad!' cried Annie. 'I'm so sorry! Now we're going to be turned into crisps on this horrible planet and it's all my fault!'

'Don't be silly, Annie. This isn't your fault and it's going to be OK! We're not going to stay long enough to turn into crisps,' said Eric firmly. 'But we do need to leave here before Alpha B rises again. Even with our spacesuits, it's too hot for us on this planet because it lies too close to its star – that's why there is no water and no life here. But we'll go somewhere else. Somewhere nicer.'

'So Cosmos can still send us further out?' said George hopefully. He didn't want to see the blinding light of Alpha B ever again in his whole life.

'Yes,' said Eric, more confidently than he felt. 'Sometimes we have to go far, far away in order to be able to get back. So don't worry if it feels like we are travelling in the wrong direction. Think of it as gaining perspective.'

'How soon will Alpha B rise again?' asked George.

'I don't know for certain,' said Eric, 'but we must be gone before its dawn.'

'Where are we going?' said Annie.

'Another planet,' Eric told her. 'Cosmos is looking for another planet to send us to. Emmett tells me that you have been following clues across the Universe – in a sort of cosmic treasure hunt.'

'Um, yes,' George admitted. 'We kept going because in each place we found another clue which sent us to a new location.'

'And you came here because the clue you found on Titan told you to go to a binary star system with a planet in orbit around one of the stars?'

'We thought we'd been really clever,' said Annie sadly.

'Oh you have!' said Eric. 'All three of you. Emmett believes that the clues are taking you on a hunt for signs of life in the Universe. If he's right, then we need to find a planet in what we call the Goldilocks Zone of its star. That means a planet that is not too hot, not too cold, but just right.'

'Oh!' said George. 'I see – this planet is too hot! So we know this isn't the right planet.'

'And I can think of another reason to suspect this isn't the right place. How many stars did the clue show?' asked Eric.

'Two,' said George.

'Here,' said Eric, 'there are three. That fainter star, the one you can only just see over there – that's Proxima Centauri, so called because it's the closest star to Earth. So this is a *triple* system.'

'Oh no! Wrong planet, wrong star system,' said George. 'What do we do now?'

'So, do you believe us now, about the clues and the messages?' interrupted Annie.

'I do, darling,' admitted Eric. 'And I'm so sorry. I'm sure those messages were left for me, not for you. And if I could send you back to Earth right this second, I would. But I can't do that and I can't leave you here. So I think we're going to have to finish the cosmic treasure hunt together. Are you with me?'

Annie moved closer to him. 'I am,' she said very definitely.

ALPHA CENTAURI

At just over four light years away, Alpha Centauri is the closest star system to our Sun. In the night sky it looks like just one star, but is in fact a triplet. Two Sun-like stars, Alpha Centauri A and Alpha Centauri B – separated by around 23 times the distance between the Earth and the Sun – orbit a common centre about once every 80 years. There is a third, fainter star in the system, Proxima Centauri, which orbits the other two but at a huge distance from them. Proxima is the nearest of the three to us.

Alpha A is a yellow star and very similar to our Sun but brighter and slightly more massive.

Alpha B is an orange star, slightly cooler than our Sun and a bit less massive. It is thought that the Alpha Centauri system formed around 1,000 million years before our Solar System. Both Alpha A and Alpha B are stable stars, like our Sun, and like our Sun may have been born surrounded by dusty, planet-forming discs.

In 2008 scientists suggested that planets may have formed around one or both of these stars. From a telescope in Chile they are now monitoring Alpha Centauri very carefully to see whether small wobbles in starlight will show us planets in orbit in our nearest star system. Astronomers are looking at Alpha Centauri B to see whether this bright, calm star will reveal Earth-like worlds around it.

Alpha Centauri can be seen from Earth's southern hemisphere, where it is one of the stars of the Centaurus constellation. Its proper name – Rigel Kentaurus – means 'centaur's foot'. Alpha Centauri is its Bayer designation (a system of star-naming introduced by astronomer Johann Bayer in 1603).

Alpha A and Alpha B are binary stars. This means that if you were standing on a planet orbiting one of them, at certain times you would see two suns in the sky!

'Me too,' said George. 'Let's finish this. And find out who is sending those messages.'

'I'm calling the portal,' said Eric. On one side of the crater, they could already see the light of dawn as Alpha B hovered below the horizon. 'Emmett!' he called. 'Any chance of a trip back to Earth?'

'Not just yet,' said Emmett. 'But I do have some reasonably good news . . .'

'You've found us a planet that might be just right, a planet about the size of Earth in the Goldilocks Zone?'

'Affirmative,' said Emmett rather weakly. 'Or at least, we've found something. It's our best guess. It's a moon, not a planet though.'

'How is Cosmos holding up?' asked Eric.

'I just want you to know,' Mabel chipped in, 'that I promised George's parents I wouldn't let him get into any trouble during the school holidays! I'm going to have a very difficult time explaining this to Terence and Daisy . . .'

'Cosmos is functioning,' said Emmett nervously. 'I've nearly finished updating the reverse portal – I'll be able to bring you in as soon as I've finished. Can you wait and I'll get you back to Earth?'

Bright rays of light were stealing across the crater, chasing the dark shadows away.

'No, we can't stay here any longer,' said Eric. 'Send us onward, Emmett. And don't worry, Mabel. We'll be back.'

THE GOLDILOCKS ZONE

Our Milky Way galaxy contains at least 100 billion rocky planets. Our Sun has four: namely Mercury, Venus, Earth and Mars – but only the Earth has life.

What makes the Earth special?

The answer is *water*, especially in liquid form. Water is the great mixer for chemicals, breaking them apart, spreading them out and bringing them back together as new biological building blocks, such as proteins and DNA. Without water, life seems unlikely.

To support life, a planet's temperature must be between zero and 100 degrees Celsius to keep the water in liquid form.

A planet orbiting too close to its home star will receive so much light energy that it will heat up to scorching temperatures, boiling all the water into steam.

Planets too far from their star will receive very little light energy, keeping the planet so cold that any water will remain as ice. Indeed, Mars has its water trapped as ice at the north and south poles.

There is a certain distance from every star where a planet receives as much *light* as it emits *heat*. That energy balance serves as a thermostat, keeping the temperature lukewarm – just right to keep the water liquid in lakes and oceans. In this 'Goldilocks Zone' around a star, any planets would stay warm and bathed in water for millions of years, allowing the chemistry of life to flourish.

Geoff

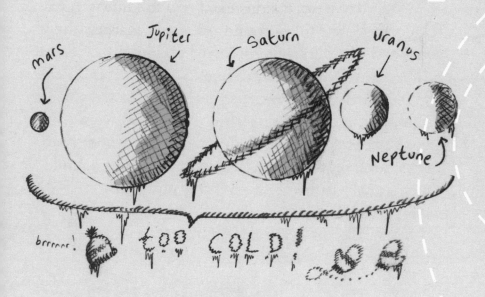

Chapter 15

Alpha B was rising as they went through the portal, shining brilliantly onto the hot, heavy planet. To avoid having to stand up again, they wriggled feet first through the doorway, with Eric hopping up as soon as he was through to pull the two kids after him.

They got to their feet and found they could stand up on the rocky surface of this new place. They didn't float off it and they weren't squished down towards it. It just felt normal – like they could move easily again, without ropes and without having to crawl around.

The light was pleasant, shining from a star in the sky that looked a bit like the Earth's Sun. It wasn't too bright, but it also didn't seem too cold – there was no ice on the rock as there had been on Mars and Titan. In the distance, they heard a gurgling, rushing sound. They seemed to be at the bottom of a rocky valley.

'What's that noise?' said Annie. 'And where are we? Are we back on Earth?'

'It sounds like water,' said George, 'but I can't see it anywhere.'

'We're in the 55 Cancri star system,' said Eric. 'It's a binary star system – the one you see shining in the sky is a yellow dwarf star, just like our Sun. Further away there is a red dwarf star as well.'

Emmett joined in from Earth. 'You are on a moon of the fifth planet around 55 Cancri A,' he said. 'The planet is in the habitable zone – the Goldilocks Zone – of its star, but the planet itself is a gas giant, about half the size of Saturn, so I didn't think you'd want to land there.'

'Well done, Emmett,' said Eric. 'I don't really feel like falling through layers of gas. Not today, anyway. You made a good choice.'

55 CANCRI

⭐ 55 Cancri is a star system 41 light years away from us in the direction of the Cancer constellation. It is a binary system: 55 Cancri A is a yellow star; 55 Cancri B is a smaller, red dwarf star. These two stars orbit each other at 1,000 times the distance between the Earth and the Sun.

⭐ On 6 November 2007 astronomers discovered a record-breaking fifth planet in orbit around Cancri A. This makes it the only star other than our Sun known to have as many as five planets!

⭐ The first planet around Cancri A was discovered in 1996. Named Cancri b, it is the size of Jupiter and orbits close to the star. In 2002 two more planets (Cancri c and Cancri d) were discovered; in 2004 a fourth planet, Cancri e, which is the size of Neptune and takes just three days to orbit Cancri A. This planet would be scorchingly hot, with surface temperatures up to 1,500 degrees Celsius.

⭐ The fifth planet, Cancri f, is around half the mass of Saturn and lies in the habitable – or Goldilocks – zone of its star. This planet is a giant ball of gas – mostly made of helium and hydrogen, like Saturn in our solar system. But there may be moons in orbit around Cancri f or rocky planets within Cancri's Goldilocks Zone where liquid water could exist on the surface.

⭐ Cancri f orbits its star at a distance of 0.781 astronomical units (AU). An astronomical unit is the measure of distance that astronomers use to talk about orbits and distance from stars. One AU = 93 million miles, which is the average distance from the Earth to the Sun. Given that there is life on Earth and liquid water on the surface of our planet, we can say that one AU or 93 million miles from our Sun is within the habitable zone of our Solar System. So for stars of roughly the mass, age and luminosity of our Sun, we can guess that a planet orbiting its star at around one AU might be in the Goldilocks Zone. Cancri A is an older and dimmer star than our Sun, and astronomers calculate that its habitable zone lies between 0.5 AU and 2 AUs away from it, which puts Cancri f in a good position!

It is very difficult to spot multiple planets around a star because each planet produces its own stellar wobble. To find more than one planet, astronomers need to be able to spot wobbles within wobbles! Astronomers in California have been monitoring 55 Cancri for over 20 years to make these discoveries.

Artwork comparing the sizes of the 55 Cancri system (left) with a small brown dwarf star system in the constellation of Chamaeleon (upper right).

The kids stretched out their arms and legs. It felt good to be able to move freely again.

'Can we take our space helmets off now?' asked Annie.

'No, absolutely not!' said Eric. 'We have no idea what the atmosphere is made of here. Let me check your oxygen gauge.' He looked at her air tank and saw that it was getting close to the red zone – running dangerously low. He looked at George's, but his was still in the green zone – plenty still in there. Eric said nothing but called Emmett again. 'Emmett, how long before we can return to Earth?'

'I'm getting hungry,' moaned Annie. 'Do you think there's anything to eat here?'

'I don't think they have restaurants at the end of Universe,' said George.

'We're not at the end of the Universe yet,' said Eric, while waiting for Emmett's reply. 'We're nowhere near. We're still really quite close to home – only forty-one light years away! We haven't even left our own galaxy yet. In terms of the Universe, this is like George coming to the States. A bit of a journey, but hardly an epic voyage.'

'What about the clue?' said George. 'Don't we need to see if there's another clue here for us? I mean, aren't we meant to be saving planet Earth from someone who wants to destroy it?'

'Hmm...' Eric was looking anxious: Emmett seemed to have gone silent. 'I think whoever sent you those messages put that bit in to scare us,' he said. 'I can't think of anything right now that is powerful enough to destroy a whole planet. It would take far more energy than we've ever generated before to blow up the Earth. That was just a threat, to make sure we didn't ignore the messages.'

'But what if it came from aliens who have sources of power we can't even dream of?' asked Annie. 'How do you know there isn't a super-race out there? Those messages weren't sent by some bacteria, were they?'

'That, I suppose,' said Eric, 'is what we're trying to find out. Annie' – his tone changed – 'why don't you sit down and have a rest? Try not to talk for a few minutes, get your strength back.'

'But I don't want to not talk,' said Annie. 'I like talking. That's what I'm good at. And football. I'm good at football. And physics. I'm brilliant at that, aren't I, Dad?'

'I know,' said Eric soothingly. 'But you're running

a bit low on air now. So I need you to be quiet for me, until we know when we're going home.'

George looked around. He studied the ravines and mountains of this rocky planet, seeking the source of the rushing noise. Suddenly, at the other end of the valley, he saw something move.

'Over there!' he said quietly to Eric while Annie sat down on a rock.

'It's moving,' muttered Eric, spotting it. 'But what is it?'

The thing was in shadow so they couldn't even make out its shape. All they could see was that it was coming towards them. It was like a black blob creeping ever closer.

'George,' said Eric, 'call Emmett *now*! Tell him we've got an ET sighting and I want him to open the portal and take you and Annie back immediately.'

'Emmett . . .' George tried to call him. 'Emmett . . . Come in, Emmett . . . Emmett, we need you to beam us up.'

The shape was approaching them along the dark side of the ravine, shaded from the rays of the yellow dwarf star, Cancri A. As it crept towards them, they noticed two tiny pinpricks of bright red light shining from its middle, like a pair of very angry eyes.

'Annie,' said Eric, 'stand up and get behind me. We have an alien approaching.'

Annie got to her feet and hurried behind her dad,

peeping round him. The black shape came closer, the red lights in its middle sparkling with demonic fury. As it approached, they could see it was shaped almost like a human being, dressed entirely in black, with scarlet eyes burning out of its stomach.

'Get back,' said Eric. 'Whatever you are, do not take another step towards us.'

The thing took no notice and continued onward. It stepped out of the shadow and into the light. And then it spoke.

'So, Eric,' its voice rasped through all their voice transmitters, 'we meet again.'

Chapter 16

'OMG!!!! It's Reeper!' shouted Annie and George at the same moment.

Standing in front of them, in a black spacesuit with a black glass visor on a black space helmet, was none other than Eric's nemesis, Dr Graham Reeper, the once-upon-a-time friend and colleague who had turned on him and become his deadly enemy.

Not so long ago, Eric had let Dr Reeper, who had been posing as a teacher at George's school, escape to start a new life somewhere else. Even though he had tried to throw Eric into a black hole and steal his amazing computer, Eric had been convinced that Reeper shouldn't be punished.

And now it seemed that Eric had made a terrible mistake. Reeper was back and – in his black suit on this distant moon – a thousand times scarier than when George and Annie had last seen him.

Reeper wasn't alone either. In his cupped hands he held what looked like a small animal with glowing bright red eyes. Its little paws scrabbled against the shiny black material of Reeper's space gloves.

'Ahhhh – look!' said Annie. 'He's found a lovely little furry pet on this planet!' She took half a step forward, but Eric shot out an arm to stop her from going any closer. The creature in Reeper's hands hissed and bared its teeth. Reeper stroked its head with one hand.

'There, there,' he said soothingly. 'Don't worry, Pooky. We'll get rid of them very soon.'

'You'll never destroy us, Reeper,' said Eric defiantly. Behind him, George was desperately trying to radio Emmett.

'Is that the boy?' asked Reeper idly. 'Is that the boy who ruined all my plans last time? How kind of you to bring him too. That's so' – the animal made a nasty growling noise – 'thoughtful. And your daughter. How charming.'

'Reeper, you can do anything you want to me,' said Eric, 'but don't touch the kids. Let them go.'

'Let them go?' said Reeper, as though considering it. 'What do you say, Pooky?' He scratched the animal's head. 'Shall we let the kids go?' Pooky hissed loudly. 'The problem is,' he explained, 'your children don't have anywhere *to* go. Or any way to get there. I know you're trying to call your dear chum Cosmos to help you out, and it's really very touching how much faith you've put in him. But you might as well save your oxygen because Pooky here is sending out a very powerful blocking signal.'

'What!' exclaimed Eric. 'What *is* Pooky?'

'Dear little Pooky,' said Reeper. 'He is my friend. Sweet, isn't he? Twice as powerful as Cosmos and so very much smaller. In fact, you could say Pooky is the nano-Cosmos. I disguised him as a hamster. After all, who would think of looking for a very powerful super-computer inside a hamster's cage?'

'What!' said Eric. 'You built a new version of Cosmos?'

'What did you think I'd been up to all this time?' sneered Reeper. 'Did you think I would just forget about everything that happened? Or did you think I would *forgive*?' He said the last word in a particu-larly unpleasant fashion. 'Forgiveness is only for lucky people, Eric. People like you. People who get every-thing they ever wanted. It's easy for you to be forgiving, with your wonderful career and your lovely family and your nice home and your helpful super-computer. You've always had everything your own way. Until now, that is.'

'Reeper, why have you brought us here?' demanded Eric. 'It was you, wasn't it, who left those clues?'

'Indeed it was,' sighed Reeper. 'At last! You guessed. It took a while though. We've been sending messages to Cosmos for ages. We began to think you would never take the bait. It's not like you to be so slow. And yes, before you ask, it was me playing games with your lovely little robot, Homer. Pooky interrupted him on the descent and managed to tamper with his programming. I thought you'd be bound to notice Homer. But no. Even that took an age. You've been terribly amateur, Eric. I expected better from you.'

'It wasn't Eric!' George stepped forward angrily. 'It was us! We were the ones who read the clues and came after you.'

'Oh, the boy wonder,' said Reeper. 'Eric's mini-me. Another disciple – how tiring.'

'Step back, George,' warned Eric. 'And keep trying Cosmos. I don't believe that nano-computer is as powerful as Reeper says.'

Reeper laughed, a horrible grating sound. 'You think you're very clever, don't you, Eric? Looking for signs of life in the Universe. But you're not as clever as me. That's why I brought you here. Finally to prove that to you.'

'Prove what?' snorted Eric. 'You're proving nothing right now, Reeper. Only that we were right to keep you away from Cosmos all those years ago.'

'Always the saint,' Reeper sneered back again. 'Wanting scientific knowledge to benefit humanity. How have you benefited humanity, Eric? Isn't your precious human race in the process of destroying the beautiful planet it lives on? Why not just help people achieve their goal faster – get rid of Earth and all those morons on it and start again? Somewhere like here. A new planet. This is what I lured you out here to see, Eric. I've completed your mission. I've found a place where life might begin – a place where intelligent life could thrive. Where, in fact, simple life could already be present.' He held up a clear phial of liquid. 'I've found *this*,' he said. 'The elixir of life.'

'You don't know that's water!' said Eric. 'You don't know what that is.'

'I do know that

whatever it is, I found it before you. *Me*, not *you*, Eric. *I* found the new planet Earth. I *own* it and I control access to it. And when the Earth finally goes *boom!* I will be in charge of the whole human race as well.'

The cosmic hamster's eyes were now glowing like a burning furnace. It scrabbled excitedly as Reeper spoke.

Eric shook his head. 'Reeper,' he said sadly, 'you are such a loser.'

Reeper howled. 'I am *not* a loser!' he said angrily. 'I am *winning*!'

'No, you're not,' said Eric. 'So you don't like humanity? So you think we've made a mess of the planet? So you'd prefer to keep all your scientific knowledge to yourself, not share it with anyone else, and perhaps charge people lots of money for the use of it? That makes you a total loser. You've cut yourself off from everything that is good or useful or interesting or beautiful – from everything human, in fact. I mean, look at your version of Cosmos. It's disgusting. And I think Pooky is moulting.'

Pooky looked outraged. Reeper rocked backwards and forwards on his space boots in fury.

Behind Eric, Annie was giving George a countdown, using the fingers of her space gloves. Silently she counted down: *Five, four, three, two, ONE!* When she got to *one*, the two kids charged forward, heads lowered, and butted Reeper in the stomach with their round space helmets.

George snatched Pooky and dashed away while Annie gave Reeper a swift kick in the tummy. Unbalanced by the sudden attack, Reeper fell backwards and lay groaning on the ground, looking like an upturned stag beetle. The phial of liquid flew out of his hand and smashed on a rock, the clear liquid seeping away. Eric ran over and put one heavy boot on Reeper's chest.

'Graham,' he said, 'this isn't why we went into science. We went into science because it's fascinating

and exciting, because we wanted to explore the Universe and find out the secrets it holds. We wanted to understand – to know, to comprehend, to write another chapter in the story of humanity's search for knowledge. We are part of a great tradition, using the work of those who went before to help us progress further and yet further across this amazing Universe in which we live. And to understand why we are here and how it all began. That's what we *do*, Graham. We bring enlightenment by *sharing* our knowledge. We don't keep it to ourselves. We explain, we teach, we seek. We move humanity forward by sharing the secrets we uncover. We aim to create a better world, on whatever planet we live, rather than finding a new world and keeping that planet all to ourselves.'

But Reeper didn't seem to care. 'Give back Pooky,' he rasped. 'He's *mine*. You stole Cosmos from me once. Don't take Pooky now. I can't live without him.'

'Pooky is only a tool,' said Eric. 'Just like Cosmos.'

'No! It's not *fair*!' ranted Reeper. 'You only say that because you have Cosmos! And you don't even need him! You can understand the Universe! I don't! That's why I wanted Cosmos, Eric. You'll never know what it's like! You've always been a genius – you don't know what's it like to be ordinary. Like me.' He started sobbing.

George was struggling to hold onto Pooky. 'I don't know how to turn him off!' he said to Annie.

'You've got to stroke his head,' she said. 'Like Reeper was doing. That's where his control panel must be.'

'I can't!' said George. 'I'll lose him – he's trying to escape! You do it!'

'Eeew!' said Annie, taking a cautious step towards him. She reached out a finger and Pooky promptly bit her. She snatched her hand back. The horrible creature hadn't pierced the space glove, so Annie was still safely sealed into her suit. She moved forward again, and this time waved one hand at Pooky; while he was watching that hand, she used the other to touch his head. She rubbed hard . . .

The next second they heard Emmett's voice once more.

'Annie! George! Eric!' he said. 'I haven't been able to get through!'

'Open the portal, quickly,' said George. 'We're coming back.'

Emmett sounded frantic. 'Cosmos doesn't have enough memory,' he said. 'He needs help. He needs another computer to join up with him to get you back.'

'Another computer!' said George. 'Where are we going to get another computer from? We're on a moon orbiting a planet forty-one light years away! It's not like they have shops here.'

Then the same thought struck George, Annie and Eric at the same time.

'Pooky!'

Reeper was still lying underneath Eric's boot, which was firmly pressing him down on the rocky surface.

'Graham,' Eric said urgently, 'we need you to help us. You must use Pooky to link up with Cosmos so we can open the portal and all go back home.'

'Send you back to Earth?' cried Reeper. 'Never! I won't help you. I've got a much larger tank of oxygen than you. So when yours runs out, I'll get Pooky off you and I'll be gone while you are stuck here for ever. By the time I come back, I doubt you'll cause me any trouble.'

Even though she knew she didn't have much air left, Annie bravely spoke up:

'Why do you hate everyone so much?' she asked him. 'Why do you want to destroy every-thing?'

'Why do I hate everyone, little girl?' said Reeper. 'Because everyone hates me, that's why. Since I was thrown out of the Order of Science to Benefit Humanity all those years ago, nothing – *nothing* – has gone right for me. It's been darkness and despair all this time. And now, at last, I'm calling the shots.'

'No, you're not,' said George. Pooky had stopped wriggling and was now snuggled up in his hands, as though about to fall asleep. His red eyes no longer glowed with menace. Instead they had turned a dim shade of yellow. 'You're just sad and bitter. And even if you leave us here and we never go home, it won't bring you any happiness. It won't gain you any friends or make you any cleverer. You'll just be alone, with your stupid hamster.'

Pooky squeaked indignantly.

'Sorry, Pooky . . .' George was growing almost fond of the small furry computer. 'Anyway,' he added, 'you knew what would happen if you broke the rules of the Order. It says in the Oath.'

'Ah, yes,' said Reeper dreamily. 'The Oath. It seems such a long, long time ago. I'd forgotten about that quaint piece of nonsense. How does it go . . . ?'

Annie started to speak but George shushed her. 'No, Annie,' he said. 'Save your air. It goes like this.' He recited the Oath he had taken to join the Order, the very first time he had met Eric.

'I swear to use my scientific knowledge for the good of Humanity.

'I promise never to harm any person in my search for enlightenment.

'I shall be courageous and careful in my quest for greater knowledge about the mysteries that surround us.

'I shall not use scientific knowledge for my own personal gain or give it to those who seek to destroy the wonderful Universe in which we live.

'If I break this Oath, may the beauty and wonder of the Universe forever remain hidden from me.

'You broke the Oath. That's why it's all gone wrong for you.'

'Is that so?' said Reeper quietly. 'And how did I come to break the Oath? Have you ever asked yourself that question? Why would I do that when I knew what I stood to lose?'

'I don't know,' whispered Annie.

'Then why don't you ask your father?' he suggested, getting to his knees. Eric had removed his foot from his chest and turned away.

'Dad?' Annie asked. 'Dad?'

'It was a long time ago,' muttered Eric. 'And we were very young.'

'What happened?' murmured Annie. She was starting to feel light-headed.

'Why don't you tell her?' said Reeper, getting to his feet. 'Or shall I? No one is leaving here until this story is told.'

'Graham and I,' said Eric slowly, 'were students together. Our tutor was the greatest cosmologist who has ever lived. He wanted to find out how the Universe began. With him, Graham and I built the first Cosmos. Cosmos was very different from how he is today. Back then, he was huge – he took up the whole basement of a university building.'

'Carry on,' ordered Reeper, 'or no one is going home. Ever.'

'Those of us who used Cosmos or worked with him formed the early branch of the Order of Science. We realized what a powerful tool we had – we needed to be careful. Graham took the Oath, and at first he and I worked together. But then Graham started to behave very strangely—'

'I did not!' said Reeper angrily. 'That is not true! You

wouldn't leave me alone. You followed me everywhere, always trying to get a look at my writing so you could copy it and pass it off as your own. You wanted to publish my work as yours and take all the glory.'

'No, Graham,' said Eric. 'I didn't. I wanted to work *with* you, but you wouldn't let me. We knew you were hiding your research from other people and we saw that you were becoming secretive. Our tutor asked me to keep an eye on you.'

'Ohhh,' said Reeper, in surprise. 'I didn't know that.'

'That's why I followed you that night – the night you went to use Cosmos all by yourself. We had a rule, then, that no one person could operate Cosmos alone. But

Graham did. He let himself into the university at night and that's when I caught him.'

'What was he trying to do?' asked George.

'He was trying,' said Eric, 'to use Cosmos to view the Big Bang itself. It was too dangerous. We just didn't know what the effects of watching that kind of explosion – even via Cosmos, even from the other side of the portal – might have been. We'd talked about it but our tutor had said no; until we knew more about the early Universe – and about Cosmos – we were not to use him to investigate the Big Bang.'

'Fools!' bleated Reeper. 'You were all fools! We could have found the cornerstone of all knowledge! We could have seen what created the Universe! But you were too scared. I had to try it in secret. It was the only way. I had to know – what happened at the very beginning of everything.'

'The risk was too great,' said Eric. 'Remember, we had sworn to harm no person in our search for enlightenment. But I guessed that was what you were trying to do – witness the first few seconds of time itself. When I followed you that night . . .'

Chapter 18

It had been a cold clear night in the ancient university town where Eric and Graham Reeper studied. The air crackled with frost and the wind bit through the thickest garments. They lived in the same college, with rooms overlooking a courtyard where the flagstones were so old that centuries of feet had worn them away. That night, the courtyard was silent, the perfect green grass turned deepest indigo by the brilliant moonlight beaming down through the velvet night sky. The clock in the tower struck eleven as Eric came in through the front gates, which were so strongly fortified it was like entering a castle rather than a place of learning.

'Good evening, Doctor Bellis,' a bowler-hatted porter said to Eric as he passed through the front lodge to collect his post. As Eric stood there, leafing through the envelopes in his pigeonhole, he caught the porter watching him. He looked up and smiled. 'You haven't dined in for a while, Doctor Bellis,' the porter commented. Fellows of this venerable institution had the right to eat off silver every night in the oak-panelled

dining room, surrounded by portraits of scholars from centuries past.

'It's been a busy time,' said Eric. He tucked his post into his battered old briefcase and wound his scarf more tightly around his neck. It was always freezing in the college, sometimes even colder than it was outside on the street, so Eric rarely took off his scarf in winter. In his rooms, it was so chilly that he slept wearing his tweed jacket over his pyjamas, along with two pairs of socks and a woolly hat.

'Haven't seen that Doctor Reeper much lately either,' said the porter, shooting Eric a look. Eric reminded himself that the porters knew everything, saw everything and heard everything. The reason he hadn't been in college much lately was because he was trying to keep up with Reeper, who was very obviously attempting to give him the slip.

'Is Doctor Reeper in this evening?' he asked casually.

'He is,' said the porter heavily. 'And funnily enough, he seemed very keen that you should know that. Something going on, Doctor Bellis?'

Eric took off his glasses and rubbed his eyes. He was so tired. Constantly tailing Reeper as well as doing his own work was becoming exhausting.

'Nothing to worry about,' he said firmly.

'We've seen it all before, you know,' hinted the porter. 'You start off friends but then you get into competition with each other. It never ends well.'

Eric sighed. 'Thank you,' he said, and walked across the main court. He slowly climbed the wooden staircase to his room and let himself in. Switching on the one-bar electric heater, he went over to the window.

On the other side of the court, he could see that Reeper's light was still on. Eric wondered if he would get a full night's sleep tonight or whether he would wake up every hour, worried that Reeper had left the college without him. He drew his curtains and sat down in an armchair. Just as he did so, the light bulb went, plunging his room into blackness. Eric just sat there for a few minutes, wondering if he could face cleaning his teeth in his sub-zero bathroom. He stood up and, on instinct, peered through a chink in the curtains, just in time to see a dark figure slipping across the courtyard, casting a long shadow in the moonlight.

Wearily, Eric put on an extra tweed jacket and left his room, carefully tailing Graham Reeper as he did a midnight flit out of the college.

Eric didn't need to follow him too closely to know where Reeper was going, but he did want to prevent him from doing too much damage. The handlebars of Eric's bicycle were covered in frost and

cycling was treacherous and slow on the icy roads. By the time he arrived at the university building where Cosmos was kept, his bare fingers were blue and numb with cold so he could hardly move them. Blowing on them, he fumbled with his set of keys and let himself in.

'What did you find?' asked George, interrupting the story in his eagerness to know what Reeper had done.

'He found me,' said Reeper, 'on the brink of the greatest discovery in the history of knowledge! And then he ruined it! And blamed me afterwards.'

Eric's suspicions had been correct. When he ran down the stairs to Cosmos's basement, he had found Reeper attempting to use the computer to watch the Big Bang. The portal doorway was already there but the door was still closed.

'I had to stop him,' said Eric. 'The conditions were so extreme at the beginning of the Universe – it was too hot even for hydrogen to form! It could have been so dangerous. I didn't know for sure what was on the other side of the door but I had to stop him from opening it.'

'But didn't you want to see?' asked George, agog. 'Couldn't you have taken a peek? Like from a long, long way away?'

'You can't view the Big Bang from a distance,' replied Eric. 'Because it occurs everywhere. What he should have done is view it with a large redshift.'

'A redshift!' exclaimed George. 'Like at your party?'

'Exactly! As the radiation emitted shortly after the Big Bang travels to us on Earth, it becomes much redder and less powerful,' explained Eric.

'But that's just what I was trying to do!' cried out Reeper. 'If you had bothered to ask me, instead of bursting through the door and tackling me to the ground, I would have told you!'

'Ahh,' said Eric slowly. Eric hadn't, in fact, given Reeper a chance to explain what he was doing. Instead, he had run into the room where Cosmos was kept and thrown himself onto Reeper who was standing near the portal doorway. In the tussle that followed, Eric had jabbed wildly with one flailing hand at Cosmos's keyboard, in the hope of shutting down the portal. But Reeper had broken free from Eric and run over to the doorway, which he had wrenched open, only to find Eric's blind strike at Cosmos's keyboard had accidentally given Cosmos the command to move the portal location to somewhere very different.

When Reeper opened the door, he found himself staring straight into the Sun. He put his hands up to shield himself from the glare but the heat burned them horribly. Weeping and moaning, he backed away as Eric got Cosmos to slam the door shut.

Eric tried to help Reeper, but his colleague staggered out of the building alone, and disappeared into the darkness. That night, it seemed, Reeper had left the university town, giving Eric no choice, he felt, but to ask their tutor to banish him for ever from the Order of Science.

'You ruined me,' said Reeper bitterly. 'You, Eric, you took everything and left me nothing. I was very embarrassed that you had caught me using Cosmos in secret. And I was in so much pain that night that I didn't really know what I was doing. I staggered out into the road and I ran – I just ran as far as I could. I must have collapsed because when I woke up, I was in hospital, half blinded by the Sun and with terrible burns on my hands. At first I couldn't even remember who I was. After a while the memories started coming back. I insisted I had to leave hospital and return to college to apologize for what I'd done. But when I got there, I found you'd had me banished, with no chance to explain myself. You'd seen to it that I could never walk into college again.'

'I was trying to protect you,' raged Eric.

'From what?' said Reeper angrily.

'From yourself!'

'Well, that didn't work, did it?' said Annie woozily. 'I mean, you've got to admit, Dad, that even though he shouldn't have been using Cosmos by himself – and we're not allowed to either, Doctor Reeper, just in case you think you're special – you did make him have a nasty accident, you didn't give him a second chance and you ended his career in science.'

'He deserved it!' said Eric. 'He knew the rules.'

'Well, only sort of,' murmured Annie. 'I mean, he didn't get to see the Big Bang, did he? After all, he was actually trying to watch it in the way you suggested but you just didn't bother to find that out! And it was you who made it really dangerous by changing the portal location. So it's at least a bit your fault.'

'My fault?' said Eric in surprise.

'Yeah,' said Annie. 'It sounds like it was just a huge

mistake and if you'd said sorry in the first place, we wouldn't be in this pickle now.'

'Say sorry?' said Eric in disbelief. 'You want *me* to say sorry to *him*?'

'Yes,' said Annie as firmly as she could. 'I do. And so does Reeper, don't you? That would make it all better. And then maybe we could get back to Earth.'

Eric mumbled something to himself.

'We didn't hear that,' George told him.

'All right, all right,' said Eric crossly. 'Reeper – I mean, Graham, I'm . . . I'm . . .'

'Say it,' warned Annie. 'And say it nicely.'

'I'm s-s-s-s,' said Eric through gritted teeth. 'I'm s-s-s-s—' He seemed to get stuck on the word.

'You're what? Exactly?' enquired Reeper.

'I'm so— so— sorr—' said Eric.

'Eric, hurry up!' muttered George. 'Annie needs to leave here.'

'Graham,' said Eric decisively. 'Graham, I'm – sorry. I'm sorry for what happened to you and for my part in it. I'm sorry I banished you without giving you the chance to explain. I'm sorry I acted hastily.'

'I see,' said Reeper. He sounded rather confused. 'You're sorry.' He didn't seem to know what to do next.

'Yes, I'm sorry!' said Eric, speaking fast. 'You were my best friend once, and my best colleague. Together as scientists we could have been magnificent. We could have done brilliant work, if only you hadn't insisted on trying to grab everything for yourself. And guess what, Graham, you're not the only person who got hurt that evening. I've missed you – at least, I missed the person you once were before you started working against me. And I've had to live with the guilt too, of what happened that terrible night. You're not the only person who's suffered. So stop being so melodramatic and get us all out of this place and back home again while we can still breathe.'

'I lost you once as a friend,' said Reeper sadly. 'And I lost my life in science. The only way I found the strength to carry on was by hating you and seeking revenge. But now, if you're not my enemy, I have nothing at all.'

'That's really silly,' said George. 'Eric has apologized and said he's sorry. Don't you think you should say something back?'

'Right,' said Reeper quietly. 'In that case, Eric Bellis, I accept your apology.' He gave a little bow.

'Your turn now,' whispered Annie.

'What?' exclaimed Reeper.

'Your turn to say sorry. That's how it works. Dad said he was sorry, now you have to apologize too.'

'What for?' said Reeper. He sounded like he genuinely didn't know.

'Oh, I don't know . . .' chipped in George. 'For stealing Cosmos, for throwing Eric in a black hole, for making us travel across the Universe because you said you were going to blow up planet Earth if we didn't. I dunno – pick your favourite and say sorry for that.'

Eric growled. 'Make it quick, Graham.'

'No need to go on,' said Reeper hastily. 'I'm sorry too. I wish I'd been a better person. I wish I hadn't wasted all that time. I wish I could go back to science – proper science . . .' He ended on a wistful, hopeful note.

'Listen, Graham,' said Eric urgently. 'You want to come back to science – fine. You want me to believe you're a good person after all – fine as well. But just get on with it and get my daughter and George back to Earth before their air runs out. Because if that happens, I can assure you that I would never forgive you and wherever you are in the Universe I will find you.'

'Do you mean it?' said Reeper. 'Can I really come back to science again?'

'Get us back to planet Earth first and then we'll talk,' said Eric.

'George,' said Reeper, 'you need to stroke Pooky on the head again. You've sent him to sleep and you need to wake him up.' George gingerly fluffed the top of Pooky's head and the hamster stirred in his hands. 'Pooky,' continued Reeper, 'I want you to link with a computer on Earth, the same computer I ordered you to block. You're going to work with him to create a doorway that can take us all back there again.'

The hamster woke up fully as George called Emmett.

'Emmett, Gran,' he said. 'Prepare the portal. We've found another computer. We need Cosmos to work with this other super-computer to make a portal powerful enough to bring us all back.'

'You found another computer? Where?' said Emmett in surprise. 'And what on earth is going on out there?'

'That's just it,' said George. 'On Earth. It's the final clue in the cosmic treasure hunt. It takes us back to where we came from. Get ready – we're coming home. Over and out.'

Pooky sat up straight and two beams of light shot out of his eyes and drew a doorway, exactly the way Cosmos did. While he was forming the portal that would carry them across the Universe, George asked a final question:

'Reeper . . .' he said as they waited for the cosmic hamster to complete the portal. 'The end of the messages – you said you would destroy planet Earth if we didn't follow them. Did you mean it? Could you really destroy a whole planet?'

'Don't be ridiculous!' said Eric, who was holding Annie as near to the glimmering portal doorway as possible so he could shove her through it as soon as it opened. 'Graham can't destroy the Earth. That would take an explosion of unimaginable power. He was just making empty threats. Weren't you, Graham?'

Reeper fiddled with his space gloves.

'Weren't you?' Eric insisted again.

'The odd thing is,' said Reeper, 'it could really happen. But it wouldn't actually be my fault. It's just something I heard about on my travels . . .'

Just then, Pooky's eyes glowed and he opened the portal doorway for them, back to the Clean Room, back to the Global Space Agency, back to the USA, back to planet Earth once more.

But this time his eyes were no longer yellow but marbled, with patterns of blue, green and flecks of white.

In his eyes shone the reflection of the most beautiful planet in the Universe – a planet which is not too hot and not too cold, which has liquid water on the surface and where the gravity is just right for human beings and the atmosphere is perfect for them to breathe; where there are mountains and deserts and oceans and islands and forests and trees and birds and plants and animals and insects and people – lots and lots of people.

Where there is life.

Some of it, possibly, intelligent.

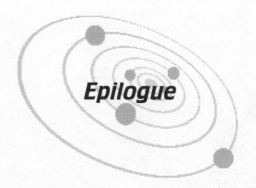

Epilogue

'Live long and prosper!' said Emmett, giving the Vulcan salute as he got into his dad's car to go home at the end of the holidays. His dad – a carbon copy of Emmett, just rather taller – grinned and took one hand off the steering wheel to give the Vulcan salute as well.

Annie and her parents, George and his grandmother all stood outside on the porch to wave goodbye.

'See you next summer!' called George, saluting back.

'Emmett, you rock!' said Annie, waving. 'Don't forget us!'

'You are firmly installed in my memory banks,' said Emmett, fastening his seat belt. 'For ever. It's been the best. I'm going to miss you.' He sniffed. 'Dad, I made some friends,' he said plaintively. 'And now I'm going to lose them again!'

'No chance!' called Annie. 'I'll be bugging you by email all the time! And so will George!'

'Maybe your friends can come and stay with us

sometime, Emmett?' said his dad. 'You know how pleased your mum would be to have your friends come over.'

'Or I could go to England!' said Emmett eagerly. 'Annie could come too and we could see George and check out some university courses over there? They do some really cool stuff.'

Eric came over to the car window. 'Well done, Emmett,' he said. 'You saved the day.'

'What day?' asked his dad. 'What have you been up to?'

'We were playing a game,' said Emmett.

'Did you win?' asked his dad.

'No one really won or lost,' Emmett tried to explain. 'We just progressed to another level.'

His dad started the car. 'Thanks, Eric,' he said. 'I don't know what you've done to my son but it seems like a bit of magic has happened here.'

''S not magic, Dad,' said Emmett in disgust. 'It's science! And it's friends. It's the two together.'

Mabel waved her cane and bellowed, 'See you at the final frontier, Emmett.'

The car drove away and the others turned back to go into the house once more. As they did so, Eric's pager bleeped, giving him news from the Mars Science Laboratory. He read the message and broke into the most enormous smile.

'It's Homer!' he said. 'He's working properly again! He's found visual evidence of water on Mars and we think it won't be long before he can send us the chemical evidence too!'

'What does that mean?' said George.

'It means,' said Eric firmly, 'that we need to have another party.'

'Are you going to invite Reeper?' asked George. 'I bet he hasn't been to a party for years.'

After they had got back from the Cancri 55 system, using Cosmos and Reeper's special nano-computer, Pooky, Eric and Reeper had spent quite some time sitting on the veranda, talking. George, Emmett and Annie had tried to listen in from the tree, but they hadn't caught much of the muttered conversation between the two former colleagues. They'd understood, however, that the conversation had ended well. Reeper had smiled at them when he came to say goodbye. Eric had found him a place at an institute where he could start studying again. It was a nice quiet place, said Eric, where Reeper would be able to catch up on what he'd missed and get involved with real science again.

The condition of Eric helping Reeper was that Pooky was left behind with Eric. Eric was going to oversee a massive system overhaul of both Cosmos and Pooky, to find out if he could link the two super-computers together. Right now, both Cosmos and Pooky were in pieces while Eric tried to work out how to do this, so there was no opportunity for any further cosmic adventures for a while.

But Eric, it turned out, wasn't the only person receiving news of life elsewhere. The house phone rang and Susan answered it, passing the receiver over to George. It was his mum and dad, calling from the South Pacific.

The satellites had spotted George's dad, a rescue mission had been dispatched to pick him up and he had returned safely to the mother ship and been reunited with George's mum.

'George!' she said on the faint, crackly line. 'We're

all safe, and we'll be seeing you and your gran soon – we're coming back via Florida. And' – she paused, as if wondering whether to continue, then went on in a rush – 'we've got some exciting news for you too! We were going to wait until we saw you to tell you, but I just *can't* not tell any longer. You're going to have a baby brother or sister! Isn't that wonderful? It means you're not alone any more. Are you happy?'

George was rather stunned. All this time they'd been looking for signs of life in the Universe and now it turned out there was going to be a brand-new life form inside his very own home.

'We'll see you in two days!' said his mum.

'Whoa!' George said to the others when he came off the phone. 'My mum's having a baby.'

'Ahh, how cute,' said Annie, smiling.

'Hmph,' said George, wondering how she would react if it was her mum and dad.

'No, it's cool!' said Annie, who'd caught the expression on his face. 'We'll have another person to join in our adventures!'

'No you jolly well won't,' said her dad firmly. 'No

babies in space, Annie. And that's a rule. In fact, no more kids in space.'

'But, Dad,' complained Annie, 'what are we going to do? We're going to be really bored!'

'You're going back to school, Annie Bellis,' her dad told her. 'So you won't have time to get bored.'

'Urrr!' Annie pulled a face. 'Can't I go and live with George?'

'Well,' said Eric, 'funny that you mention it. I was thinking of taking you back to England. Now that Homer works properly and he's found water on Mars, it might be time for me to take part in another great experiment that's in progress in Europe – in Switzerland. We could all go back to the house in England and I could join the work from there easily.'

'Yeah!' Annie and George celebrated together. They wouldn't have to be apart again.

They all wandered out onto the veranda, wondering what to do with themselves now that all their challenges were over and Emmett had left.

George picked up *The User's Guide to the Universe*, which was lying on the garden table. 'Eric,' he said thoughtfully, 'there's something I've been meaning to ask you but we haven't had time until now.'

'Go on,' said Eric.

'When we were' – George lowered his voice – 'out there, Reeper said something. He said that you understood the Universe. Is that true?'

'Well, yes, it is,' said Eric modestly. 'I do.'

'But how do you do that?' said George. 'How does that happen?'

Eric smiled. 'Turn to the last pages in the book, George,' he said. 'And there you'll find the answer.'

HOW TO UNDERSTAND THE UNIVERSE

The Universe is governed by scientific laws. These determine how the Universe starts off and how it develops in time. The aim of science is to discover the laws and to find out what they mean. It is the most exciting treasure hunt of all because the treasure is the understanding of the Universe and everything in it. We haven't found all the laws yet so the hunt is still on but we have a good idea of what they must be in all but the most extreme conditions.

The most important laws are those that describe the forces.

So far we have discovered four types of forces:

1) The Electromagnetic Force
This holds atoms together and governs light, radio waves and electronic devices such as computers and televisions.

2) The Weak Force
This is responsible for radioactivity and plays a vital role in powering the Sun and in the formation of the elements in stars and the early Universe.

3) The Strong Force

This holds the central nucleus of an atom together and provides the power for nuclear weapons and the Sun.

4) Gravity

This is the weakest of the four forces but it holds us to the Earth, the Earth and the planets in orbit around the Sun, the Sun in orbit around the centre of the Galaxy, and so on.

We have laws that describe each of these forces, but scientists believe that there is one key to the Universe, not four. We think that this division into four forces is artificial and that we will be able to combine the laws that describe those forces into a single theory. So far we have managed to combine the Electromagnetic and Weak forces. It should be possible to combine these two with the Strong force but it is much more difficult to combine the three with gravity because it bends space and time.

Nevertheless we have a strong candidate for the single theory of all forces that would be the key to understanding the Universe. It is called M-theory. We haven't completely worked out what M-theory is, which is why some people say the M stands for 'mystery'. If we do, we will understand the Universe from the Big Bang to the far distant future.

Eric

INDEX TO SPECIFIC FACTUAL SECTIONS

There is lots of science within this book, but there are also a number of separate sections where facts and information are provided on specific subjects. Some readers may wish to refer back to these pages in particular.

ACKNOWLEDGEMENTS

This book comes with our grateful thanks to:

Jane and Jonathan, without whose kindness and support this book would not exist. William, for his sweetness and good humour about his mum and grandad writing another book.

Garry Parsons, for his illustrations which capture the storyline, the adventure and the characters so perfectly.

Geoff Marcy, for his amazing lecture at the Institute of Astronomy in Cambridge which inspired the theme of this book.

The distinguished scientists who made their work accessible to a young audience through the essays that form *The User's Guide to the Universe*. They are Bernard Carr, Seth Shostak, Brandon Carter, Martin Rees and Geoff Marcy. Their expert knowledge and enthusiasm for this project made it a joy to work on.

Stuart Rankin at the University of Cambridge, for writing so brilliantly about how light and sound travel.

Our friends at NASA and all the people in the different departments who took the time and trouble to talk to us about what NASA does and how it works. In particular, we would like to thank Michael Griffin, Michael O'Brien, Michael Curie and Bob Jacobs.

Kimberly Lievense and Marc Rayman at the Jet Propulsion Laboratory in California, for their help with the wonders of robotic space flight.

Kip Thorne and Leonard Mlodinow at Caltech, for their advice and friendship.

Richard Garriott and Peter Diamandis at Space Adventures, for their energy and enthusiasm, and Richard for including us – and the first George book – in his real-life space adventure! Thanks to him, *George's Secret Key to the Universe* has now visited the International Space Station.

Markus Poessel, for his attention to detail and helpful comment.

George Becker and Daniel Stark at the Institute of Astronomy, Cambridge, for their invaluable comments.

Sam Blackburn and Tom Kendall, for patiently answering endless quirky science, engineering and computing questions.

Tif Loehnis and all at Janklow and Nesbit, UK, for their kindness and hard work on the George series. And Eric Simonoff in the New York office, for sending George to the USA once more.

At Random House, our wonderful editor Sue Cook, for her tremendous work which brought the Cosmic Treasure Hunt together and made it into such a beautiful book. Lauren Buckland, for her great work on the text and the images; Sophie Nelson, for the careful copyedit; and James Fraser, for his wonderful front cover. Also Maeve Banham and her team in the Rights department, for helping to ensure that the George books truly do reach an international audience. And a special thank you to Annie Eaton, for her dedication and warmth towards the George series.

Keso Kendall, for her help with how a teenage super-computer should speak.

All the 'team' – at home and at the University – for their patience and generosity towards another 'George' book.

Finally but most importantly, we would like to thank our young readers – Melissa Ball, Poppy and Oscar Wallington, Anthony Redford and Joanna Fox, for their thoughtful feedback and their very helpful comments on the Cosmic Treasure Hunt. And we would like to thank all the kids who asked the questions, who wrote, emailed, or came to lectures and were brave enough to stand up and ask something at the end. We hope this book gives you a few answers. And we hope you never stop asking 'Why?'

Lucy and Stephen Hawking

About the Authors

LUCY HAWKING is the author of two novels for adults and has written for many British newspapers as well as appearing on television and radio. Lucy has given popular talks on space travel and science for kids all round the world, including a talk at NASA's 50th birthday celebrations in the USA. Her DNA recently went into space as part of 'Project Immortality'. It is now kept on the International Space Station in case the human race accidentally perishes. Lucy is the winner of the Sapio Award for Popularizing Science 2008. She lives in Cambridge with her son.

STEPHEN HAWKING is the Lucasian Professor of Mathematics at the University of Cambridge. He is widely regarded as one of the most brilliant theoretical physicists since Einstein. His adult book *A Brief History of Time* has been a phenomenal bestseller worldwide and is now available in more than 30 languages. His latest book for adults, *The Grand Design* (with Leonard Mlodinow) is available from October 2009.

About the Illustrator

GARRY PARSONS studied Fine Art at Canterbury and went on to study illustration at the University of Brighton. His work has won him several prizes, including the 2004 Red House Children's Book Award for his picture book, *Billy's Bucket*. Garry lives in London.

Join George in another dimension at
www.lucyandstephenhawking.com

Explore even more of the Universe,
access exclusive content, enter
competitions, test your
knowledge and register
for free George updates!